THE SHORT-TIMER

THE SHORT-TIMER

A Story of Love and War

Dennis D. Skirvin

DEO GRATIAS
Thanks be to God

I dedicate this book to the American soldiers who served in Vietnam— especially those who gave their lives.

I also dedicate it to the brave, selfless men and women of our armed forces who fought and died for our nation during the many years of conflict in the Middle East. Their sacrifices and struggles stand as profound examples for all Americans.

Finally, I dedicate it to a genuine rebirth of the American spirit and to a clearer understanding and appreciation of our history.

ACKNOWLEDGEMENTS

To my wife and family for their love and support.

To Anthony Bernardo, PhD for his help and support on an earlier, unpublished version of this work.

To Robin Hill-Page Glanden for her superb editing.

To Lt. Sean E. Finerty (Ret.)
Crisis Management Tactical Team
Wilmington Police Dept., Wilmington, DE
(I interviewed Lt. Finerty in the 1990s, after first starting this book.)

AUTHOR'S NOTE

The Short-timer: A Story of Love and War is a work of fiction. Nevertheless, I could not have written it without having served in Vietnam as an Army infantryman. I conceived the idea for this novel in the mid-1990s and went to work on it. I copyrighted that first version in 1997. During the summer of 2021, I took it out of storage and went back to work on it, with the intention of making it a better story. After much re-writing and with the help of a talented editor, I finished the manuscript in August of the following year.

It is my hope that readers not only find it an interesting and intriguing story, but that it provides them with a far better understanding of the many stresses combat veterans face on their return to civilian life.

Dennis D. Skirvin

GLOSSARY OF TERMS

Vietnam

Arty	Artillery
ARVN	Army of the Republic of Vietnam (friendly soldiers)
Babysan	A Vietnamese baby or child
Beat feet	Move out in a hurry, run
Beaucoup	Many, a lot (French)
Believer	As in "make a believer", to wound or kill the enemy
Boom-boom	Intercourse, sex
Boonies	Back country, deep jungle
Bush	Back country, deep jungle
Case of the ass	Angry, upset, mad about something
Charlie	The enemy, VC, NVA
Chi-Com	Chinese Communist
CP	Command Post
C rations, C rats, Cs	Canned food that soldiers carried
Di-di, Di-di mau	Move out quickly, run
Dung lai	Stop
Dust-off	Medical evacuation helicopter (chopper)
Freedom Bird	The airliner that carried soldiers home
Ground-pounder	U. S. Infantryman
Grunt	U. S. Infantryman
Hooch	A structure made of wood, grass, sticks, sandbags, or any combination of those elements
KIA	Killed in Action
Klick	1,000 meters, one kilometer, 0.62 miles
Mamasan	A Vietnamese woman
Number One	Good
Number Ten	Bad
NVA	North Vietnamese Army (enemy soldiers)
O.D.	Olive drab color
Old Heads	More experienced soldiers, with more time in-country
Old Man	The Commander of a company of infantrymen
Papasan	A Vietnamese man
PF	Popular Forces (friendly)

RF	Regional Forces (friendly)
Roger (Rog)	Yes, affirmative
RTO	Radio Telephone Operator, radio man
Saddle up	Get your gear on and be ready to move out
Shaming	Feigning sickness or injury to get out of work
Short-timer	A soldier who has little time left to serve in-country
Smoke-bringer	Someone who brings havoc on the enemy
The World	The United States of America
Un-ass	Leave in a hurry, get up, get out
Viet Cong	Vietnamese Communist, VC, Victor Charlie, Charlie.

Spanish

Amigo	Friend
Ay, caramba!	My gosh, oh my God!
Dios mio!	My God!
Hijole!	Wow! Son of a gun!
Madre mía	My mother
Muchas oraciones	Many prayers
Mucho	Much
Nada	Nothing
Ni hablar!	No way!
Oye!	Listen up!

My soul finds rest in God alone;
from Him comes my salvation.

Psalm 62

Table of Contents

CHAPTER 1

Wilmington, Delaware
Friday, February 22, 1991—Day 37 of the Gulf War.

In his cramped duplex apartment on the city's west side, in the shadow of the steeple of a nearby Catholic church, 42-year-old Brian Scott sat alone in a living room armchair. His television was tuned to CNN, where commentators spoke ceaselessly about the situation in the Gulf—

Flying a record number of missions, the American-led allied forces stepped up their bombing attack on Iraqi positions inside Kuwait. A Marine was killed in ground combat and five others were wounded. President Bush countered a Soviet peace plan with an ultimatum, and America held its breath as the long-awaited ground offensive drew closer.

Excited analysts went on to paint a series of possible scenarios with a palette of dire colors, while outside the apartment, a cold, rainy sleet tapped against the troubled Vietnam veteran's windowpanes. Scott, however, was not so focused on the weather, the commentator's predictions of casualties, or even the intermittent ringing of his telephone.

Instead, a derisive inner voice gripped his attention with a monotonous rehashing of the costly errors and difficulties that had soured his young life. He was familiar with the belittling voice and

had learned to ignore it as best he could, or at least to let it talk itself
out. In recent weeks, however, that voice had become more constant,
more insistent and emphatic, and its sting spread a demeaning,
crippling poison into his spirit. Now, it focused almost entirely on
the greatest chink in the armor surrounding his fractured ego, the
grievous thing he had tried so hard and for so long to wipe from his
memory. Like a cat toying with a mouse, it wouldn't let go. The
stifling guilt and remorse he had pushed into a deep, dark hole and
buried, had burst free and metastasized into his heart and soul. Deep
within this black funk, Scott pointed his .45 at the television set. The
.45, the .45 … he remembered it—

The air reeked of napalm and putrid flesh. Under a merciless sun,
dead NVA soldiers lay black and bloated in the jungle high ground.
Scott stood over the bullet-riddled body of one of the fallen.
"Way to go, Brian," a buddy said, "you made a believer out of
this sorry son-of-a-bitch!"
The grunt picked up the dead man's AK-47 rifle, and Scott took
a .45 semi-automatic and holster from his web belt. The weapon
looked like U. S. Army issue, but was somehow different. *Chi-Com*,
he wondered, stashing the souvenirs into his rucksack.

"It's your fault, Scott," the voice said. "All your fault. Death's no
big deal, man, nothin' but a long, peaceful sleep. Do it, man! It
would be better than what you have now."
With an unsteady hand, he raised the pistol to his head. The cold
steel of the muzzle brushed his ear. Tears cascaded down his cheeks
and fell onto his lap like rain drops. Shaking badly, he nearly
dropped the gun. Then the voice spoke again, taking him back in
time—

"Hey, Scott, how many babies did you kill over there in
Vietnam?"
A gang of workmen relaxed in the dim factory lunchroom,
drinking coffee and smoking. A haze of cigarette smoke clouded the
room like a fog at dawn. Scott choked down his anger and searched

his pockets for change. It was not the first time he had heard the insult.

"Come on, man, how many kids you kill?" the voice laughed, trying to break him.

"Leave the guy alone," another called.

Scott suddenly noticed that his dirty, jungle fatigue pants were ripped wide open from knee to thigh and that swollen leeches were feeding on his leg. He dropped a quarter into the vending machine and stood in the hot Vietnamese sun sipping coffee from a paper cup. His clothes were soaked with stinking sweat. Dropping his rifle onto the lunchroom floor, he helped his comrades lift body bags onto the chopper. The spirits of the dead spoke to him. One of the bags unzipped itself and Raul, looked out at him.

"*Oye*, Brian!" the ashen-faced corpse said, "don't take any shit from that sorry ass punk!"

The voice turned heckler again, putting a dagger into his heart and twisting it. "Fuckin' baby killer … fuckin' baby killer ...'"

Enraged, Scott hit the wise guy square in his jaw, wiping away his smirk and knocking him to the floor. He turned his .45 back to the TV, where the white-haired boss spoke to him.

"You're fired, Scott!" he said, angrily. "You've given me no other choice. Fighting is inexcusable. Get your things and get out." The elderly man's soured look suddenly turned to a grin. "We know about you, Scott—and the Short-timer. Now go on, get out!"

The Short-timer!

On the television, a senator talked with a CNN reporter—but Scott only saw his two ex-wives going on bitterly about him, how he had wrecked their lives because of some inner turmoil he had brought into their marriages. Then, the sweat-soaked face of the Short-timer stared at him from afar.

"Fuckin' new guy!" he cursed. "They shoulda hanged your sorry ass."

In his consciousness, a long file of soldiers moved past him, stealthy and half-blind, through a murky jungle night. Once more, he heard their muffled curses, groans, and complaints, wishing he

3

could go back and live that night all over again, to have one more chance to make it right! The sleep-starved grunts trudged on through the blackness. "Keep contact, keep moving!"

Scott struggled for a reason to spare his life. He placed the .45 to his temple and rested his finger on the trigger. On the stand, next to the television, a photo caught his eye. *Kathy! Oh, God in Heaven, Kathy!*

But the voice intruded, urging him to drive out the pain once and for all. "Pull the trigger, man. You owe it to him. Pull the trigger."

CHAPTER 2

Wilmington VA Center (Hospital)—Elsmere, Delaware

Kathy Hamilton, a thirty-five-year-old brunette and single mother of one young son, pulled her car off of busy Robert Kirkwood Highway and turned into the VA Center, where she worked in the hospital as a Physical Therapist. She followed the winding entrance road around to the rear of the sprawling complex, which was built in 1946 on a beautiful, 32-acre grassy site. She parked in the lot, jumped out of her car, and entered the hospital through its west entrance. It was Friday, 7:30 in the morning. For some reason, a nervous anxiety hung over her, and with it, a nagging feeling that something was wrong.

Going into the Occupational Therapy & Physical Therapy Clinic, she quickly stashed her handbag and coat in her office and stepped back out into the corridor, going toward the valet entrance. She could hear the hubbub of people coming in and going out of the hospital, but she was on a mission and didn't stop to talk with anyone. Rounding a corner and going past the Chaplain's Office, she neared the valet entrance, then turned right, and walked up the short hallway to the chapel.

Kathy Hamilton had been born and raised Catholic, but like many others of her age, she had fallen away from the faith and stopped going to Mass altogether. In short, she had lost faith in God and had steered her life onto a completely secular path. All that changed, however, nearly nine years ago when her comfortable world was suddenly turned upside down by an unexpected, life-changing event—an unplanned pregnancy. It was the result of a brief love affair with a charming, yet deceitful man, a virtual stranger, who blew in and out of her life like a torrid, summer heat wave. He swept her off her feet, and left her pregnant and alone to fend for herself. That devastating betrayal, her poor judgment, and the birth of her son had a profound effect on her.

As the shock and bitterness began to recede, she stopped blaming the world for her misfortune. In the process, she took a hard, critical look at her life and the path she had chosen. The introspection led her back to truth, and finding great consolation in God. Kathy came home to Him like a prodigal daughter. It was wonderful and so inexplicably strange how the seemingly catastrophic set-back had come to fill her with such love and incredible joy upon the birth of her son Zach! Now, as a single parent and Catholic re-vert, she believed that God had a plan in everything, and she evinced a great faith and trust in Him, both of which played a meaningful part in her life.

Entering the mid-sized, multi-denominational chapel, the noise and distractions of the busy hospital and the outside world faded immediately. Here, the atmosphere was calm and serene. She genuflected toward the wooden altar, made the Sign of the Cross, and took a seat. With folded hands and lowered head, she skipped the formal prayers and spoke to her Maker directly, silently, and in her own words, telling Him of the terrible anxiety that had suddenly come over her. It was a brief, heartfelt, and honest talk. Finally, in a tearful petition, she asked Him for wisdom and understanding, and to show her the path to wellness. She ended with an earnest, "Amen!" then quietly returned to the clinic.

. . .

At 10:10 a.m. she was busy at her office desk completing a patient's paperwork, when her phone rang. "PT, Kathy Hamilton speaking," she answered.

"Hey, Kath, it's Julie—got time for a quick coffee?" It was Julie Benedict, head nurse on 4E, and one of Kathy's best friends.

6

Kathy glanced at her watch and hesitated. "Well, I don't know ...

"Oh, come on! Meet me in ten. It's crazy up here today, and I need a caffeine fix."

"Okay, but I can't stay long. I'm busy here, too."

"Must be something in the air. See you in ten. Gotta run."

Going back to her work, Kathy envisioned hectic 4E at this time of the morning and knew that the daily rat race was in high gear. The med-surgical floor, where patients ranged from acute care to neuro and spinal injuries, had a reputation for a frenetic pace.

. . .

There were only a few people in the second-floor cafeteria when Kathy went in looking for Julie. No sooner had she gotten coffee and taken a seat, than Julie rushed in.

"Hey, sorry I'm late," the attractive blue-eyed blond said, sitting across from Kathy and setting her coffee on the table. "I would have been here sooner, but Mr. Flannigan—he's the neuro patient I told you about the other day—well, he decided to go for a little stroll without his pajamas. We found him near the elevator, naked as a newborn."

Julie shook her head and laughed. At 38-years-old, she looked younger. Only the little crow's feet at the corners of her bright eyes belied her youthful looks. "Oh God, it's been a heck of a day," she added, sipping her coffee and fidgeting with the stethoscope hanging at her neck.

Kathy nodded with a smile. Then with her hands around her coffee cup, her expression suddenly darkened. "Have you heard any news?" she asked.

"About?" Julie tilted her head slightly and set her cup down.

"The war. Anything new?"

"No, I haven't really had time to listen. But the patients have been glued to their TVs and radios, that's for sure. They're very keyed up over it. I'm sure it's bringing back a lot of memories. The media has been going on about it all day. I don't think the ground war has started yet, but you get the feeling it could happen any minute. I

7

hope it's a short war, and I hope they get *Insane Hussein*. What a case!"

Listening intently, Kathy glanced away.

"Hey, you seem a little down today. Anything wrong?" her friend asked.

"No, things are fine," she said thoughtfully.

But Julie wasn't buying it. She'd known Kathy too long not to notice when she was upset about something. "Come on," she said, "out with it. What's buggin' you?"

With a sour expression, Kathy faced her friend. "It's Brian! I'm worried about him."

Julie leaned closer. "What's wrong with him?" She took a quick sip of coffee and stared intently at Kathy.

"I'm not sure," she stammered. "But suddenly he's become moody and withdrawn. It's so out of character. I've never seen him like this." She paused, then added, "It's just strange—and really upsetting."

"Moody and withdrawn. What do you mean?"

"I can't exactly explain it. The other night we went to Leonard's, the restaurant on Union Street, and during dinner I got up to use the rest room. When I came back, he was crying."

"Crying! Are you sure?"

Kathy nodded, looking as if she might cry herself. "His eyes were red with tears from crying. I asked him what was wrong, but he couldn't tell me. I think I embarrassed him, catching him like that."

"Now, that is strange, Kath," Julie agreed. "Did he ever tell you why?"

"No," Kathy said. "And I didn't bring it up again."

Julie sipped more coffee. After a moment, she asked, "What in the world could be troubling him?"

Kathy paused before going on. "Well, you know we've been dating for almost a year and a half now and it's been great. Since my pregnancy, I didn't think I could trust someone again, let alone fall in love, but Brian has proved that all wrong. Not long ago he asked me to move in with him."

"You said yes, I hope?" Julie interrupted.

Kathy shook her head and leaned back in her chair. "No," she said. "I told him I couldn't."

"For cryin' out loud, Kath, you and your old-fashioned values!"

"Old-fashioned or not," she replied, defensively, "I'm not the person I once was. Besides, my situation is different from yours. I have a son to think about, a son who's going to be a teenager in just a few years. No, I couldn't, it just wouldn't be right. I told Brian that and I think he understands, but I'm not sure."

Julie nodded sympathetically. "Could there be anything else troubling him?"

"His welding work has slowed down some," Kathy shrugged. "But I don't think that's it. You remember I told you he runs his own business?"

"Yes, I remember."

The two turned silent as three maintenance men walked past them, on their way to a table. When they were out of earshot, Julie resumed. "I hear what you're saying, Kathy, but honestly, none of this sounds so bad, at least not bad enough to affect him in the way you're describing. You sure there's not something else, something you might be missing?"

Frowning, Kathy sat back in her chair. "There could be something, but I'm not sure. It's just a feeling I have."

"What is it?"

"It's this war with Iraq," Kathy declared. "Maybe it's affecting him? It started back in August, and that's when I first noticed a change in him."

"You might be on to something," Julie said. "Isn't Brian a Vietnam veteran?"

"Yes, but he's not one to talk about it. Maybe occasionally he'll mention something, but as a rule he's quiet about Vietnam. Anyway, he's been overly interested in this war and extremely critical of it."

"Well, he's not alone. The whole country is worried and anxious. You think that's upsetting him?"

"It's sure possible," Kathy said. "Maybe it's triggered something. Maybe it's a post-traumatic thing. I don't know." She fell silent, thinking. In a moment, she went on, "You know he's been through

9

two marriages, and he's had job problems before opening his business. So, I'm looking at him and thinking to myself—how can all this happen to such a good guy? Now I'm beginning to see another side of him. And I'll tell you something else …" Kathy's hand suddenly jerked forward, knocking into her cup and jostling coffee onto the table.

Julie grabbed a napkin and dabbed up the spill. "Calm down, Kath," she said. "You're getting upset."

But she couldn't calm down and went right on speaking. "I love Brian and won't let anything happen to him." Her face was flushed with worry.

Julie smiled. "Hey, I believe you'd whip the devil for that man." She took her friend's hand and squeezed it gently. Leaning back, she gulped the last of her coffee, then glanced at her watch. "Uh-oh! I gotta run! You could be right about Brian and the war. Let me talk to Arthur about it tonight. I'll see if we can't get a professional opinion."

Arthur was Dr. Arthur Benedict, Chief Psychologist at the hospital, and Julie's husband of five years.

"Oh, Julie, that would be great," Kathy said, sounding hopeful. "I was going to ask if you would."

"Hey, what's a pal for? Didn't you mention earlier this week that you're working tomorrow?"

"Yes, every now and then I work a Saturday to catch up on my computer work, and tomorrow's the day. So, I'll be here."

"And so will I," Julie said. "In fact, Arthur's going to be here for a while in the afternoon. He's coming in for paperwork, I think. I'll ask him to stop by to see you."

"Oh thanks, Julie. You're a peach!"

Outside the cafeteria, the two women hugged, then parted company. "See you tomorrow," Julie called, rushing toward the elevator. "And don't worry. I'm sure there's a simple explanation to what's going on."

Kathy took the stairs down to the ground floor. Back in her office, she quickly telephoned Brian's welding shop, then she tried his

10

apartment again, but each time there was no answer. She tapped her pen against the desktop, wondering, *What in the world is going on with Brian?*

CHAPTER 3

After work, Kathy left the hospital and drove east toward Wilmington along the heavily congested Kirkwood Highway. A light rain continued to fall. Invisible patches of ice plagued motorists like hidden booby traps, slowing movement to a crawl in places. She continued to a commercial section of town close to the Christina River, where warehouses and shipyard businesses once thrived. Now the area was marked by dozens of empty, tumbledown properties. Ahead lay the darkened silhouette of Scott's Welding Shop.

"No lights, no pickup truck," Kathy murmured to herself. "He's not here!"

Turning around and switching on the radio, she headed for his apartment while listening to an all-news AM station, where a commentator, an ex-military general, was opining on the impending ground war. Minutes later, she switched it off again. *More doom and gloom!* she said to herself. *It's no wonder veterans are getting upset.*

She drove in silence, growing more and more apprehensive. On reaching his apartment, she saw his pickup parked by the curb. *Thank God!* she sighed, feeling somewhat relieved. The sidewalk leading to the apartment was slippery with ice. Going cautiously to the porch, she found her key, and let herself in.

Brian sat in the front room, slumped in his armchair in the dark. The TV was on and tuned to CNN, where a roundtable of commentators discussed the war.

"Brian!" she said. "Where have you been?" She closed the door behind her. "I've been calling you all day, since early this morning. I've been worried sick about you."

He glanced up at her, squinting. "I've been right here, watching TV. Didn't feel like going in to work today."

She looked confused. "I don't understand. Just a few days ago you said your schedule was filling up again with more jobs coming in."

Brian shrugged.

"Why haven't you answered my phone calls? Is your phone out of order?"

He shrugged again and turned back to the television.

She walked into the adjacent dining room, picked up the receiver and listened for a dial tone. "It seems to be okay." She dialed the number of the neighbor's home where Zach stayed after school.

"Hi, Mrs. Brinkman, this is Kathy ... Yes, everything's fine. Tell Zach I'll pick him up in twenty minutes or so. Something came up and I had a quick errand to run. Sorry, I should have let you know ... Okay, thank you ... Good-bye."

She turned to Brian. Something wasn't right, but what? Whatever could be causing this strange behavior? The irritable, disheveled figure in the chair was not the vibrant, confident man she knew and loved. Watching him, she felt her hands trembling.

"I don't understand," she finally said, brushing her hair back out of her face. "If you were here all day, why didn't you answer the phone?"

Swiveling in his chair, Brian snapped at her, "I told you I never heard the phone! If I had, I would've answered it. Don't make a big deal out of it. I never heard it, okay—so let it go." He shifted uncomfortably in his seat.

"That's not good enough, Brian!" she replied, crossing the room to the front window. "And why is it so dark in here?" She pulled the curtains aside to let light in from the streetlamp outside, then she switched on the end table lamp to brighten the room even more. "Now, tell me what's going on?"

13

Ignoring her, he averted his eyes from the light, and shifted in his chair. A dark shadow covered his square jaw where he had neglected to shave, and his dark blond hair draped uncombed over his forehead.

"What's wrong?" she pleaded. He made no reply. "Did you forget about dinner tonight?" She stood staring, waiting for an answer, some explanation. "Brian, look at me. I'm talking to you. Quit staring at the TV and answer me! Did you forget about dinner?"

He seemed to emerge from a trance. "What? What dinner?" he said, sounding confused.

"We had planned to take Zach out for pizza tonight. Remember? It's Friday."

"I forgot all about it. Sorry"

"Well, it's not too late. Why don't you take a shower and meet me at my place? We've got time."

Brian shook his head. "No, no, I'm not up for it. Tell Zach I'm sorry and couldn't make it. I just don't feel like it." He turned back to the television.

Kathy felt herself getting more upset. "Brian," she pleaded again, "what's wrong? Why are you acting so strange? Something's wrong. What is it? Tell me!"

He turned toward her. "There's not a damned thing wrong with me. Just because I'm not up for pizza, suddenly there's a crisis." He got up from his chair, pointed at the TV, and shouted, "If anything's wrong, it's this damn war! Now they're sending troops to the desert to kick hell out of some third-rate, ass-backward country just to keep the oil flowing. Body bags for oil barrels. Some sorry exchange! Nobody gives a rat's ass about the troops—just like before."

Kathy clasped a hand over her mouth and pressed back against the door. She had never seen him so enraged, so upset, and it frightened her. Sudden tears moistened her eyes, and her hands and knees trembled. She sat down on the couch to think. Finally, after getting herself together, she said in a calm voice, "I'm worried, Brian. You're not yourself. This is not you. Something is wrong. Tell me what's bothering you?"

"There's nothing wrong," he grumbled, eyes back on the TV. "Not a thing. And I'm not upset."

Patiently, she waited a few moments. "I don't believe you," she finally said. "I know you well enough to know that something is troubling you. Tell me what it is, please!"

He sat back down, lowered his head and buried his face in his hands.

Kathy went to him and put a soft hand on his shoulder. "I love you," she pleaded. "I love you so much." She let the words sink in, then in a soothing, persuasive tone, continued, "Talk to me, Brian? Does it have anything to do with Vietnam?"

The word *Vietnam* ignited a firestorm in him. He jumped up in a rage, startling her.

"What happened to me in 'Nam is none of your business," he shouted. "It's my business and mine alone."

Kathy got out of his way as he stormed to the clothes tree by the door. "You can stay here all night," he said, "and nag someone else for all I care. I'm going out."

He grabbed his field jacket and put it on as he went back to his armchair. Turning his back to her, blocking her vision, he secretively pulled his .45 from between the seat cushion and the arm rest and put it into a jacket pocket. Without a word, he went out, angrily slamming the door behind him.

Kathy stood in shock, crying and wiping tears from her eyes, while the TV spewed more predictions of the coming carnage in the Gulf. She found the remote and switched it off, wishing she could switch off the war, too. Scared and worried, she sunk into Brian's armchair trying to make sense of it all. It was so strange, so inexplicable, so out of character for him. Sobbing, she lowered her head into her hands and prayed, asking God once more to help her understand what was going on with him and to keep him safe. It was a solemn, sincere prayer. When she finished, she glimpsed something shiny on the carpet by the chair. Picking the small object up, she gasped, "A bullet!"

To the best of her knowledge, she didn't know if Brian owned a gun or kept one in his apartment.

. . .

Mrs. Brinkman was quick to answer her doorbell and greeted Kathy with her usual bright smile and good humor. "Oh, come in, Kathy," the elderly woman said, opening the door and letting her in out of the sleet and rain. "It's just terrible out there. Not fit for a snowman."

"Sorry I'm late. Something very important came up after work and it just couldn't wait."

"Everything is all right, I hope," the woman said, as her mood turned serious. "You have a worried look about you." She brushed her snowy-white hair back from her forehead and straightened her glasses.

"No, everything's fine," Kathy fibbed.

The woman shot her a look of doubt. "Are you sure?"

Kathy nodded. "Yes, nothing to worry about. Is Zach okay?"

"He's fine!" she said with a smile. "I hear you're taking him out to dinner tonight. He's eager to get going!"

"Pizza," Kathy replied.

On cue, Zach ran in from the rec room, where he had been watching television. His long-sleeved white shirt was a wrinkled mess and his blue necktie hung sloppily from his collar. Zach was in the sixth grade at the nearby Christian school and still in his uniform

"Hi, Mom," the youngster said, giving his mother a hug. "Hey, is Brian coming with us tonight?"

Choking back her emotions, Kathy replied, "No, I'm afraid not, Zach. He's just too busy tonight with work."

"But he said he was," the boy complained.

Kathy smiled. "Well, I understand your disappointment, but sometimes things just don't work out as planned. Brian will join us another night soon. Don't worry."

He seemed satisfied with the answer, and in moments he was cheerful again. Kathy told him to get his jacket on and stay by the door for a moment.

"Wait until I get the car started. It's miserable out and I don't want you getting a cold."

Mrs. Brinkman agreed. "Your mother's right! Get your coat on and wait right here." She turned to Kathy, and said, "I'll send him out in a few minutes."

Kathy nodded. "Thank you." Then she gave Zach a warning. "Be careful coming outside, it's very slippery."

"No sweat, Mom," he said.

After Kathy started her car, she flashed her lights and Mrs. Brinkman let Zach out. He raced down the sidewalk wearing his backpack, paying no attention to his mother's warning about the slippery conditions.

It was a short drive to their two-story brick home in the suburbs of Wilmington, near the General Motors Boxwood assembly plant. Pulling up to the house, Kathy told Zach, "Put your bookbag away and change your clothes. When you're ready, we'll go for dinner."

After she opened the front door, he rushed into the house, dropped his backpack on the floor and made a wild dash for the kitchen. On the way, he carelessly knocked into an end table, causing a favorite photograph of Kathy's to fall onto the floor.

"Get back here!" she shouted, and when he had hurried back, she said, "Pick up your bookbag and take it up to your room. No running. Change your clothes and we'll go in a few minutes."

Frowning, he picked up his bookbag and raced upstairs. "No running," she called after him. Shaking her head, she watched him disappear, then straightened the end table and picked up the photograph, noticing that the frame was still intact, but the glass was cracked. But it was the photo itself and not so much the minor damage that suddenly grabbed her attention. Looking at it, she recalled the story behind it.

It was Wednesday, July 4th, 1990—a bright, sunny day filled with love and hope of a happy future. Kathy had the day off, and Brian closed his shop for the holiday. They had slipped away together to southern Delaware, to beautiful Rehoboth Beach, to enjoy a day at the seashore.

17

Like the two lovers they were, Brian and Kathy sat side-by-side on a boardwalk bench next to the railing and faced the pristine, blue-green Atlantic Ocean. Close by, squawking seagulls made a racket as a man threw popcorn into the air and the birds squabbled over each airborne piece. Brian raised his arm from Kathy's shoulder and glanced at his watch. "Hey," he said in surprise, "it's almost noon! No wonder my stomach's growlin'. Whoever said 'time flies when you're having fun,' was right." He pulled her close and kissed her.

"So, you're having fun," she said, with a grin.

"It doesn't get any better." He kissed her once more.

Two little girls, standing by the railing with their parents, giggled and pointed at the lovers. Noticing them, Brian got an idea. "Hey, let's give 'em something to really laugh over!" he chuckled. With no warning, he wrapped his arms around Kathy, leaned into her, and gave her his best Hollywood kiss. The girls giggled and laughed again, but their parents weren't nearly so impressed. They pulled their daughters away and resumed their stroll along the boardwalk.

Red-faced with embarrassment, Kathy broke free with a laugh. "You're too much, Brian," she said, straightening her hair. "Too crazy."

"What's crazy about showing how much I love you? And I don't care who knows it!" He kissed her again. "Now, what do you say we get something to eat? I'm half starved."

They quickly joined the holiday crowd on the boardwalk, and headed for Grotto Pizza Restaurant, a popular Delaware pizza joint. But on making their way, an elderly man in front of them collapsed and fell. Brian rushed to his aid.

"Stanley, Stanley!" a stout, gray-haired woman screamed in shocked surprise at her unconscious husband. "Oh my God! Oh my God!"

As a crowd formed, Kathy took her by the arm. "It's all right," she said, comforting her. "He'll be okay."

Brian loosened the old man's shirt collar and checked him over. "His breathing and pulse are fine," he said.

"Maybe it's the heat," Kathy said, as the man's wife looked on. "It's really hot out here."

18

Brian pleaded with the crowd of onlookers to move back. "Please, everyone, back up and give this poor guy some room to breathe."

Kathy coaxed them back as well. Brian spotted a man with a beach umbrella, and calling him closer, asked if he'd open it to shade the unconscious man. He quickly complied and some others in the crowd helped hold up the umbrella.

Brian sent a boy to nearby Grotto Pizza to ask them to make a 911 ambulance call. In a few moments, the day manager, a heavyset man in a white apron, with arms dusted white with flour, appeared with a jug of cold water. Brian unbuttoned and loosened the man's shirt even more and dabbed water onto his forehead and lips with a napkin.

After a few minutes, the man began to revive. "He's coming around," Brian said, excitedly, noticing he had opened his eyes.

"Thank God!" the man's wife cried. "Thank God." Kathy gave her a reassuring hug.

Two policemen pushed through the crowd and ordered everyone to move on. As one officer coaxed the bystanders to move away, the other knelt next to Brian.

"I think he fainted," Brian quickly told the policeman. Then, the veteran gave him a brief, eye-witness account of the incident.

The officer appreciated the information. "Okay, and thank you," he said, sincerely. "You've been a big help, buddy. Now, we'll take it from here."

But Brian wouldn't hear of it and wouldn't budge. He insisted on staying close to the man, cooling him with the water.

When the man's color began returning, the policeman spoke to his wife. "I don't think he'll need that ambulance. It's probably just a case of too much sun. I'm going to cancel it."

Brian was quick to disagree. "No," he said, sternly. "Beebe Hospital is just a few miles away in Lewes. He had a pretty good fall. It won't hurt to have him checked out." With the man's wife and Kathy agreeing with Brian, the policeman quickly relented.

By the time the ambulance arrived, the victim had regained his wits. "I feel okay!" he cried. "I'm not going to any hospital."

19

"Listen to your wife," Brian told him. "You need to be checked. It's the smart thing to do. You just never know."

Finally, the obstinate old man gave in, and as the ambulance crew wheeled him to their waiting vehicle, his wife quickly introduced herself to Brian and Kathy.

"I'm Charlotte Robinson," she said. "My husband and I are here on vacation. I can't thank you two enough for your kindness."

Brain and Kathy smiled. "We're glad we could help," Kathy said.

"Let me get a picture of you two," she insisted, pulling a little camera from her handbag. "I want to show them at home that there are still many good people left in this world."

Brian objected, but Kathy sweet-talked him into it. Together, with their arms around one another, they smiled for the picture.

The woman took Kathy by the arm and in a sincere whisper, told her, "Give me your address and I'll send you the picture. Hold on to that man of yours. He's a good one, with a good heart!"

Knowing it to be true, Kathy smiled. "Thank you," she said as she wrote her home address on a slip of paper in her handbag.

A few weeks after the incident, Kathy received a large envelope from the woman and two copies of the photo she had taken of them on the boardwalk. Kathy had the pictures framed and gave one to Brian, which he kept in the front room of his apartment by the television set. The photo had come to be very special to them both.

CHAPTER 4

It was shortly after 7:00 p.m. when Kathy and Zach returned home from dinner. All through their meal, Kathy was preoccupied with worry. She simply could not shake the dreadful feeling that Brian was hurtling toward a crisis, and she was almost certain the catalyst was the Gulf War. *It has some connection with his time in Vietnam*, she thought. *But what?* She didn't know and could not even venture a wild guess—but she was determined to find out and avert any impending crisis, and the sooner the better.

Wasting no time, she made a quick phone call to Mrs. Brinkman. Thankfully, she was home and graciously agreed to come over and watch Zach. She arrived at 7:30.

"Oh, I can't thank you enough," Kathy said to the kindly sitter, putting on her coat. "Another matter has come up and I just have to take care of it. I'll be back as soon as I can."

Mrs. Brinkman looked a bit skeptical. "Are sure you are ok, Kathy?" she asked. "You're not in any kind of trouble, are you? You seemed worried earlier tonight when you picked up Zach. And now this. What's going on?"

Kathy shook her head. "I'm not in any kind of trouble, but there is something wrong. And I'm trying to get to the bottom of it as quickly as I can. That's all I can tell you right now. That and thank you so much for coming. Now, I've got to run!"

Mrs. Brinkman nodded. "Ok, but be careful. It's still messy out."

Kathy thanked her and darted out the door.

. . .

She drove into Rodney Manor, a sprawling mobile home park in nearby Stanton, where Brian's father lived. She recalled Mr. Scott as a tall, obstinate, opinionated man, and a reclusive widower who seemed perfectly content in his bitterness. Since knowing Brian, she had rarely heard him talk about his father, and had correctly surmised that they were not very close.

A huge, sprawling oak at the end of tree-lined Selby Drive sparked her memory. The double-wide mobile home was at the far end of the street, on the corner. She parked in front and walked the curved sidewalk to the porch. Country music came from within. Knocking, she pulled her collar up to better shield herself from the wind. In a moment, the music stopped and the door swung opened. Mr. Scott peered out at her.

"Mr. Scott," she said in a raised voice. "It's Kathy Hamilton, Brian's friend." The wind suddenly gusted across the open porch. Kathy clutched her coat at the neck.

Mr. Scott opened the door a crack. "Who are you?" She could see he was smoking.

"Kathy Hamilton. I'd like to talk with you about Brian."

He held the door open for her, and she stepped inside. "Come in," he said. "Of all nights to come out." He shook his head testily. "Let me have your coat." Kathy said she was cold and preferred to keep her coat on, but she also thought it would be a good idea in case her visit ended abruptly.

In the living room, he pointed to a leather sofa, and said, "Please, have a seat."

She sat on the edge of the sofa and quickly surveyed the room. It was larger than she remembered it. The odors of ham, cabbage, and cigarette smoke permeated the room. Mr. Scott stood watching her, smoking a cigarette. "Can I get you anything? Coffee?"

"No thank you. I don't have much time." Under his watchful eye, she felt uncomfortable, and she shifted nervously.

"Well then, it must be important for you to come here, especially on a night like this. What about Brian? Is he alright? Get to it."

22

"I'm very worried about him, Mr. Scott," she said, brushing her dampened hair back from her forehead. "He's been acting strange lately and hasn't been himself. I first started noticing it back in the fall, soon after the Gulf War got going."

Mr. Scott stiffened. "What in the name of God has the Gulf War got to do with Brian?"

His tone made her feel even more apprehensive and uneasy. She crossed her legs nervously. "Nothing directly, I'm sure. But perhaps indirectly it's affecting him. I don't know. I'm just guessing. He's been bad-tempered and brooding about something. And it's so unlike him. Earlier tonight, I asked him about Vietnam, and he exploded. I'm very worried about him."

Brian's father sat across from her in a chair. He stared critically at her as he snubbed out his cigarette in an ashtray and quickly lit another.

"Can you tell me anything about his tour in Vietnam?" she continued. "Was there anything unusual? Did he ever talk to you about it?"

He took a deep drag on his cigarette and exhaled slowly. The pungent, gray smoke settled between them like a wall. "I'm not sure what you want to know."

"I'm not sure either," she replied. "I'm looking for something, anything that might explain what's going on, and maybe the troubles Brian's had in his life, too. It could all be related."

Exhaling, Mr. Scott blew more smoke into the room. "I'll tell you what I think about his troubles," he said, curtly. "They all boil down to poor judgment. That's right, poor judgment! He got himself tangled up with a couple of women who had different ideas about what marriage is all about. And I'll tell you another thing, the very last thing he needs now is another woman in his life and another marriage." Finishing, he sat back in his chair with an angry scowl on his weathered face.

Irritated by the remark, Kathy boiled over. "Maybe I made a mistake coming here," she snapped. "I don't know what your problem is, Mr. Scott, but there is something wrong with your son, and I think it goes back to something that happened to him in

23

Vietnam, and this terrible Gulf War is bringing it back in a bad way. If you love Brian, you'll listen to me and help. But if you won't tell me anything or can't tell me anything, I don't have any time to waste." She got up from the sofa.

"Hold your horses," he said, motioning her to sit back down. After a few moments, he softened and said, "Brian very rarely spoke about his tour in Vietnam, and his mother and I never asked him about it. It was just something that wasn't discussed." He leaned back and took another long, thoughtful drag on his cigarette.

"One night many years ago," he resumed, "like so many other nights back then, I had been drinking and arguing with Brian's mother, God rest her soul. I was going on and on about Brian, the war and Vietnam veterans—how they were a bunch of whiners who were responsible for our nation's only defeat." Looking down at the floor, he paused momentarily. "I don't know what got into me," he began again, sorrowfully. "Anyway, most regrettably, Brian had come in unbeknownst to us, and he overheard me. Of course, I apologized to him and said it was just the bottle talking." Filling up with emotion, he stopped again. "I don't think he ever forgave me. Anyway, when you see him, tell him I said hello and to stop around. Will you do that for me?"

"I will, Mr. Scott. I'll be sure to tell him."

"I'm eighty years old, and don't have much life left in me, Miss Hamilton. I'm a war veteran myself, World War II. I fought the Japanese in the Pacific and I have my own demons to deal with."

"I'm sure you do."

For a few moments, neither of them spoke. Then the old man suddenly thought of something, and his face lit up.

Noticing a change in him, she asked, "What, what is it?"

"I don't know if this will help, but when Brian first came home from the war, he had a rough time adjusting. You know he went from the jungle to home in just a few days. And like I said, he rarely spoke about it. His year away was very rough on us as well, especially his poor mother. We worried constantly. But it made her sick, literally sick. She's a casualty of that damn war too, and so am I!" With a darkened look, he quieted to think and reminisce.

"During those early days after his return, he had a lot of problems sleeping at night, and when he did finally fall off to sleep, he sometimes talked in his sleep. More often, it was incoherent Army stuff about this squad or that platoon and so on. But some nights he repeated things that were kind of strange ... even chilling. I still remember."

"What things? What did he say?" Eagerly, Kathy sat back down on the couch.

"He'd toss and turn in his sleep as if in the throes of some terrible nightmare memory, and when he got like that he'd talk about a long, eerie file of shadowy soldiers moving through the darkness, about being alone ... and then, every time, he'd cry out the same two names—the Death Ray and the Short-timer! I could never forget them because they were so odd."

Kathy struggled to make sense of it. "The Death Ray and the Short-timer?" she said, sounding confused. "I don''t understand. What do they mean?"

"I have no idea, probably code names for someone or some operation. But whatever they meant, they were very upsetting to him because he'd always wake in a sweat, with tears in his eyes."

"Did you ever ask him about them?"

The old man stiffened. "No, neither of us did. It was none of our business. It was something for him to work out. After a while, he stopped with the restless nights, and we never heard anything more about it. I always felt like I had been eavesdropping just knowing about it. It's often best to let sleeping dogs lie, Miss Hamilton. Promise me you won't go rooting around in Brian's past, stirring up things and getting him worked up!"

"It's too late for that," she said, standing. "Your son is already worked up. I can't promise you anything. I intend to find out what's wrong with him and if it takes getting into Vietnam, so be it. I intend to help him—it's about time someone did! Now, I've got to be going. Thank you for your time. If you think of anything else, anything, please call me. My number's in the book."

Mr. Scott escorted her to the door. "When Brian was in Vietnam," he said, "he won the Bronze Star for bravery. Did you know that?"

"No, I didn't," she said.

"The Bronze Star," the old man mused. "I've always been proud of him."

Opening the door, Kathy stood silent for a moment, looking at him. Finally, she said, "When's the last time you told him that, Mr. Scott?"

Lighting another cigarette, he watched her walk to her car. In the darkness, he saw the rain falling past the streetlamp. He thought of the Pacific and the bloody island fighting. But as Kathy Hamilton got into her car and drove off, his thoughts turned to Vietnam—and his son.

CHAPTER 5

On leaving Mr. Scott's home, one thought churned in Kathy's troubled mind: *Tomorrow can't wait*! Again and again, in her lonely desperation, she repeated the words, until she pulled into a nearby convenience store to call Julie Benedict. *I have to speak to Arthur tonight.*

Timber Woods was a new, custom-built housing development in the posh Hockessin area west of Wilmington, which was once known for its beautiful rolling hills and open farmland. A building boom during the 1980s, however, helped by an influx of financial institutions into the state, blanketed it with new developments and some of the nicest homes in Delaware.

Kathy turned onto Timber Road and followed it to number sixteen, the Benedicts' two-story English Tudor home. Julie waved from a side entrance door as Kathy pulled into the wide driveway and got out of her car. She held the door open for her friend as she jogged through the rain.

"Hurry, come in, Kath. Get out of this cold rain." Julie gave her a hug when she came into the kitchen and took her coat.

"It's so kind of you to let me stop by like this," Kathy said. "I know it must seem kind of strange and a bother but …"

Julie waved a hand, cutting her off. "Not another word about it, Kathy. It's fine! Now, come on. Arthur's in his study"

Taking Kathy by the hand, she led her through the kitchen, into a hallway, and into Dr. Benedict's study, where they found the forty-five-year-old psychologist sitting in a large winged-back chair, with his head erect and his eyes closed in quiet meditation. An open book rested on his lap and a glass of red wine sat in easy reach on a small table at his side. Classical music came softly from an FM radio station. He opened his eyes and stood the moment the two came into the room.

"Kathy," Arthur enthused, "it's so good to see you." He greeted her with a soft handshake and a peck on the cheek. In a tan sports coat and white turtleneck, he cut quite the handsome figure.

"It's nice to see you, Arthur. Thank you so much for meeting with me on such short notice. It's very kind of you."

"Nonsense. Come in and have a seat. Would you care for a glass of wine?"

"No thank you," she replied. "Not tonight."

He showed her to a seat on the sofa. Julie quickly sat down next to her.

"Now," he said, going back to his chair, and picking up his glass, "tell me what this is all about. Start at the beginning. What's going on with Brian?"

Kathy related everything she could think of that pertained to Brian's situation—the things she had noticed since the beginning of the Gulf War, detailing his odd behavior the entire time, and concluding with his sudden blowup earlier in the evening.

"Is it possible," she questioned him, "that the war with Iraq has somehow stirred up his Vietnam memories, maybe painful memories, and they're responsible for his sudden change in behavior?"

Arthur Benedict did not hesitate. "Indeed, it's quite possible! In fact, at the hospital, I've been seeing an increased level of anxiety among many of the patients. With your experience at the VA, Kathy, I'm sure you're familiar with Post-Traumatic Stress Disorder."

Kathy nodded. "Yes, I'm aware of it, but as a physical therapist, I'm not as knowledgeable as I could be. But I wouldn't be surprised if Brian's been suffering with it for years. It could explain his two broken marriages and his employment difficulties. It could explain a lot of things."

"PTSD is a complex phenomenon," the learned psychologist said. "Combat veterans often get it in an acute or chronic form. It's also known to strike after a long delay, sometimes years. Sufferers can become anxious, alienated, and very depressed. Vivid flashbacks, aggressive behavior, difficulties with relationships—these are all symptoms of the disorder."

Julie spoke up, "I know that survival guilt also figures into it."

Arthur nodded. "Yes. Many veterans feel guilty about surviving while others, often close friends, died. Kathy, your points about Brian's failed marriages and his job history fit into the pattern. You don't suspect he's a drug user, do you?"

"No. I'm sure of it. He'll hardly touch a beer." She moved to the edge of the sofa, rubbing her hands together nervously.

"That's a plus," Arthur declared. "A substance abuse situation only makes the problem more difficult to deal with. Now from what you have described, Brian could very well be suffering with PTSD, but maybe not. You could be misreading the situation. Is there anything else going on that could be the cause? I understand he has a welding business in Wilmington, could that be the problem or perhaps something in his relationship with you?"

Kathy shook her head. "No! There's nothing I can think of that would make him so angry and so interested in the Gulf War. Everything was fine between us; his welding business had fallen off some, but it's picking up again. I don't see it as the cause. He's proud of his business and he's worked hard at it." She suddenly began to choke with emotion. "No, it's Vietnam! I know it is. I feel it in my gut."

Julie leaned close, took her friend's hand, and squeezed it gently. "I think you're right, Kath. I think it's Vietnam, too."

"Before I came here tonight," Kathy said, "I visited Brian's father and told him what's going on. At first, he didn't seem concerned—he's a hard man. But he told me some things about Brian and the war."

"What did he say?" Arthur asked.

29

Kathy related how Brian had once overheard his father criticizing Vietnam veterans, blaming them for having lost the war, and how those comments caused a rift between them.

"Well, that's certainly significant," Arthur said, mulling over the information. "Did his father tell you anything else that might be pertinent?"

Kathy hesitated, then finally said, "He did tell me something, but I don't know if it's relevant or not. It's sort of strange."

Arthur's interest was immediately piqued. "What was it? What did he say?"

Kathy proceeded to tell him what Mr. Scott had said about Brian's trouble sleeping when he first came home from the war, and on further questioning from Arthur, she mentioned his bad dreams and the two strange names he often repeated while in the throes of those nightmares.

"The Death Ray ... the Short-timer," Arthur mused. "Are you sure that's what he said?"

"Yes, I'm positive. The names were so strange, I couldn't forget them."

Julie turned to her husband. "A short-timer, isn't that what the soldiers called someone who had only a short time left in Vietnam?"

"Yes, it's slang, but normally meant as something positive, a good thing," Arthur said. "Most of the soldiers in Vietnam had a one-year tour of service. Marines served thirteen months, so when a soldier got down to his last month or last couple of weeks or days, they called him a short-timer. Perhaps Brian was referring to himself, or a close friend." Arthur shrugged. "It's hard to say."

"But what about the Death Ray?" Julie asked, looking confused. "Whatever could that mean?"

"That's a tough one," Arthur admitted. "I have no idea what it means or refers to. Perhaps it was a code word for an operation, or a nickname for a unit or a weapon. I really don't know."

"Maybe they both have something to do with what's troubling Brian?" Julie said, grasping for an answer. "Maybe they're the memories that have brought on PTSD."

"I'm afraid we could go on speculating like this all night," Arthur pointed out. "I think the best thing you can do for him, is to get him to the VA on Monday. That's what I would recommend."

With an affirming shake of her head, Julie agreed. "Arthur is absolutely right," she said. "It's the first step. If you're going to find out what's going on, the starting point is a thorough evaluation."

"Exactly," Arthur concurred, after taking a sip of wine. "We've got a full slate on Monday, but I'll make sure to squeeze him in. We'll get to the bottom of this. If it's PTSD, we'll get him on medication and regular visits. But, as Julie pointed out, the first step is a thorough evaluation."

The Benedicts seemed pleased with the plan, but Kathy still had reservations. "That's fine," she said, "but I can't shake this sinking feeling that something bad is about to happen—something terrible and soon."

"Why?" Arthur asked. "What makes you feel that way? Has Brian said or done anything that gives you the impression he may harm himself or someone else?"

"No, not exactly," she stammered, "but you didn't see him like I did, just sitting there, staring at his television, totally absorbed, like he was in a trance, taking in every word about the Gulf War. It was frightening. I'm just so worried about him."

"Veterans suffering with this illness can be frightening," Arthur pointed out. "It's very worrisome to their loved ones."

Kathy nodded, then went on. "Before leaving his apartment tonight, I was so upset I sat and cried, trying to get a handle on all that had happened. As I was sitting there, I found this on the floor." She held up the squat little bullet, then handed it to Arthur.

"If I'm not mistaken, it's a .45 caliber cartridge," he said, looking it over closely. "You found this in his apartment?"

Kathy nodded. "Yes, just a short while ago, on the floor by his chair. And Brian's not a gun guy. He's not a target shooter or hunter. I've never heard him talk about guns. I don't think he even owns one."

"Well, this definitely adds a twist to things," the doctor said, "but it still doesn't prove that anything is wrong or that there is an imminent danger. I still believe the best course is to keep a good eye on him and at the same time to get him to the VA on Monday. His cooperation will certainly make things go easier. But if he refuses, I'd be willing to visit him at his apartment, provided you come along, too."

"Thank you, Arthur, I can't tell you how much I appreciate what you're doing. I suppose that's all we really can do." Kathy stood up.

Julie stood and hugged her friend. "Try not to worry so much about this. Everything will be fine. You'll see."

"I hope so. I won't let anything happen to him."

"Tomorrow afternoon I have some work to do at the hospital," Arthur said. "I'll stop by your office and drop off some information about Post-Traumatic Stress Disorder. It'll give you a better understanding of what we may be up against."

"Thank you so much, Arthur. You're so kind."

During the drive home, Kathy decided to go by Brian's apartment to see if he had come home. On the radio, the war news repeated that the ground war was imminent. Switching it off, she thought, *Damned war. Damn them all! It's like an addiction that has hooked every generation. It only brings death and suffering. When will the madness ever stop?*

On reaching Brian's block, she looked for his pickup but didn't see it anywhere. *He's not home. Where can he be?*

Later that night at home, when Zach was sleeping soundly in his bed, she tiptoed into his room and gave her son a kiss on the forehead. Before leaving his room, she stood by his bedside, looking down at him sleeping so peacefully. She whispered an earnest prayer that he would never have to go off to fight in some terrible war. The mere thought of it, sent a tremor of fear up her spine.

CHAPTER 6

Saturday, February 23, 1991—Day 38 of the Gulf War

By 7:00 a.m. Kathy had already been up for over an hour. Her night had been a restless one, filled with worried tossing and turning. *What if? ... what if?* She kept asking herself the same question, and each time, a new and even more troublesome scenario came to mind. Mrs. Brinkman arrived at seven-thirty before Zach was up. Kathy welcomed her in, then rushed off to work.

She parked and entered the hospital through its west entrance as she did each day. Before going to her office, she went to the chapel. She sat silently praying that the Lord would relieve Brian of his stress and anxiety and lead him out of the darkness he had wandered into. It was an earnest, sincere, and heartfelt petition from the heart. When finished, she remained seated in the comfort of the peaceful room, decompressing, and letting the burdensome fear and worry diminish. After a few minutes, when she felt better, she got up and left for her office.

In the hallway, she met the Chaplain, Reverend Dario Renzetti, who was unlocking his office door.

"Good morning, Kathy," he said, with a look of surprise. "What are you doing here on a Saturday?"

"Catch up work, Father Dario," she replied with a grimace. "So many patient forms. It's hard to keep up with it all during regular hours when we're treating patients."

Father Dario nodded sympathetically. "I understand. It's a common complaint. We used to call it paperwork, now it's computer work." He paused, then noted, "I see you're coming from the chapel. Early morning prayers?"

"Yes, Father."

The good priest stood watching her, waiting for her to say something more, but when she didn't, he said, "Well, I'll leave you to get to your work. Have a nice day."

She smiled and started up the hall, but didn't get far, before she stopped and turned back. "Oh, Father Dario!"

He stuck his head out of his office doorway. "Yes. Is there something I can help you with?"

Kathy came nearer. "Yes, there is something, Father."

The heavy-set priest stepped into the hall. "I'm at your service, Kathy. What can I do for you?"

With a sudden grim look of worry, she paused, then explained, "I have a friend, Father, a dear friend and veteran, who is going through a very troubled time. I was wondering if you might include him in your prayers. Would you, Father?"

The old priest smiled. "I'd be more than happy to pray for your friend. What is his name?"

"Brian," she quickly said. "Please pray for Brian!"

Nodding, Father Renzetti took her hand. "I will indeed pray for him. I hope it's nothing life threatening?"

Sorrowfully, Kathy said, "PTSD! I'm almost certain."

"That's a rough one," he admitted, "but with the proper help, and prayer, it can be overcome." Suddenly, his serious look brightened. "Wait here a second," he said. "I have something for you."

Going back into his office, he searched through his desk for something. On finding it, he returned to her with a smile. "Here, take this," he said, handing her a simple prayer card. "Put all of your fears and worries into the hands of our merciful Lord and Savior," he advised. "Trust in Him alone."

"Thank you, Father," she said, giving the card a cursory look. "I greatly appreciate it." She put the card into her pocket for safe keeping and left for her office. Moments later, seated at her desk, she took out the card and read the short *Divine Mercy* prayer:

Eternal Father, in whom mercy is endless and the treasury of compassion inexhaustible, look kindly upon us and increase Your mercy in us, that in difficult moments we might not despair nor become despondent, but with great confidence submit ourselves to Your holy will, which is Love and Mercy itself. Amen.

. . .

Kathy worked undisturbed for most of the morning. Every half hour or so, she telephoned Brian's apartment and welding shop, but got no answer. Julie called around 11:00 a.m., and even though it was the weekend, she complained that things were still busy on 4E. Just before noon, the two met in the cafeteria for lunch.

"Heard anything from Brian?" Julie asked her friend, as they sat down at a table.

"Not a word," Kathy said, dejectedly. "He's not answering his phone, and I don't know where he is or what he's doing, or even if he's okay. This is so nerve wracking, and so strange."

"I know it is, Kath," Julie said sympathetically, "but just hang in there. No news is good news, as they say."

Kathy looked doubtful. "I'd rather know what's going on."

"Soon enough you will. Arthur will figure this out. He'll take good care of Brian. He's an excellent doctor, and he's very worried about Brian—and you. Now, take a deep breath and try to relax. Let's enjoy our lunch."

Kathy forced a half smile.

. . .

Later that afternoon, Kathy was just finishing a phone call when Arthur Benedict walked into her office carrying a manila envelope.

"Have you heard from Brian yet?" the doctor asked.

"No," she grumbled. "I was just trying to reach him. He's not answering his phone, either at home or at his shop. I have no idea

35

where he is." Leaning back in her chair, she threw her pen onto her desk.

"Don't despair," he said, with an encouraging smile. "He'll turn up."

Looking doubtful, she muttered, "I hope so."

In his crisp white lab coat, Arthur stood by the edge of her desk. "I can see how upset you are, but you have to relax. At this moment, there's not a thing we can do, or anyone else can do, for that matter. If you're not careful, you'll worry yourself sick."

"I know, I know," she admitted. "But it's a lot easier said than done. I just wish I knew where he was!"

Arthur nodded. "That's understandable." He handed her the envelope. "Here's the PTSD information I promised you. It provides a very good overview. After you've looked it over, call me if you have any questions."

He paused for a moment. "When you do catch up with Brian, be sure to tell him about Monday. Get him in here so we can figure out what's going on. Remember, if it's PTSD, it's very treatable." He glanced at his wristwatch. "I'm sorry I don't have more time, but I really have to get back."

Kathy got up from her desk. "Thank you so much for your concern, Arthur, and for the information. I will certainly read through it." She came around her desk and walked him out.

Arthur stopped by the doorway. "Now promise me you'll relax," he said.

"I'll do my best."

"That's good enough. And promise me one more thing, too."

"What's that?"

"If you need help, you'll call me or Julie right away."

"I promise," she said.

"Good." He nodded with a smile, handing her his card. "Take this. It has my pager number, just in case you can't reach me. And be sure to let me know about Monday. I'll jockey my schedule to make time for Brian."

Kathy assured him that she would, and thanked him again for all his help. Going back to her desk, she opened the envelope and read over the PTSD literature.

Before leaving for the day, Kathy tried calling Brian's apartment and his shop again, but as before, her calls went unanswered. It was shortly after 5:00 when she pulled out of the parking lot. On the radio, Sinatra sang one of her favorites, his crossover hit, *"Strangers in the Night."* The sweet melody and tender lyrics quickly swept her back to October 1989 and the night she first met Brian.

She was at a Halloween party thrown by a co-worker and his wife. Everyone was in costume. Kathy was dressed as a gypsy fortune-teller in a fetching, low-cut dress, big hoop earrings, and a lacy scarf around her head. Brian came as a western sheriff, complete with cowboy boots, ten-gallon hat, oversized badge, and a shiny cap pistol hanging on each hip.

A noisy crowd had lined up in the hosts' dining room, awaiting their turn at a smorgasbord of food spread over the table. Kathy stood in line talking with the party hostess when someone suddenly bumped her from behind. She turned to see Brian in his western get-up. Someone from behind had accidentally bumped him into her.

"Well pardon me, little lady," he apologized, doing a very poor impersonation of John Wayne. Then politely tipping his big hat, he added, "These pilgrims in here are gittin' a little rowdy."

She couldn't help laughing at him, and his ridiculously large hat. Her laughter was infectious. It made Brian and the hostess laugh, too. The hostess excused herself and Kathy and Brian exchanged introductions and got acquainted.

About an hour later they met again. Kathy had stepped out onto the back deck to get some air. It was a beautiful, starry night, with just a bit of a chill in the air. Music from a nearby radio tuned to an FM station played softly. Brian seemed to appear out of the dark. *He has the most wonderful smile,* she thought.

"I love your outfit," he said, pushing his hat back. "You look terrific. But I've been trying to figure out who you're supposed to be?"

She laughed, then struck a melodramatic pose. "I am a mysterious gypsy fortune teller," she purred. "I can see the future."

Brian chuckled. "Where's your crystal ball?"

"Don't need one!" she declared. "That's movie stuff. Genuine fortune tellers can see the future without corny props. I only have to look into a person's eyes."

"Okay," he quickly replied, moving closer, "then look into mine and tell me if there's a beautiful fortune teller in my future?"

Kathy blushed. After a brief pause, in which they quietly looked closely at one another, she coyly replied, "There could be."

On the radio, Frank Sinatra sang so touchingly of *two lonely people, these strangers in the night*. The song, indelibly etched in this fondest of memories, became her favorite, while Brian became much more than that—he became the special someone she loved with all her heart and soul.

. . .

When Kathy reached home and pulled into her driveway, she saw Mrs. Brinkman standing in the front doorway, as if she were waiting for someone. Alarmed, she parked and rushed to the front door, which the sitter quickly pushed open.

"Is everything all right?" she asked. "Is Zach okay?"

"He's fine," Mrs. Brinkman replied. "He's in the basement playing with his trains."

Kathy dropped her briefcase and handbag in the foyer.

"Everything's fine," the sitter said, "but you just had a phone call from Mr. Scott."

"From Brian?"

"Yes," she replied. "When I told him you weren't home, he asked me to give you a message."

"What message?" The words rushed out of her. "What did he say?"

"He said to tell you that he loved you and Zach very much. I was surprised that he would tell me that. He didn't sound at all like himself."

Feeling faint, Kathy leaned back against the wall to steady herself. Her world was unraveling, spinning out of control.

Mrs. Brinkman continued, "Are you okay?"

"Yes, yes. Did he say anything else?"

"No, that's all he said," she explained. "What's wrong, Kathy? You look so worried."

"I am worried. Something is going on with Brian." She fought back tears as she tried to get her thoughts together.

"Is he sick?"

Kathy ignored the question and asked, "How long ago did he call?"

"I just hung up with him this minute, just before you pulled up."

"Did he say where he was calling from?"

"No," she said, shrugging.

Kathy turned to leave. "I've got to go back out. I'm sorry, but I must. I'll explain all this later. I'm very worried that something terrible is going to happen. Can you please stay with Zach for a while longer?"

Mrs. Brinkman nodded. "Sure, I'd be happy to. You go on."

Kathy ran to her car, and headed to Brian's apartment, hoping to find him there. Speeding dangerously, she weaved between the slower eastbound traffic on Maryland Avenue, a major artery that led directly into the city. Passing cars and switching lanes, she soon reached the Cleland Heights residential area along South Lynam Street, where a stop sign forced her to a standstill just one block from Brian's apartment. Up ahead, she saw him come out of his apartment. He was wearing his Army field jacket.

Thank God! Thank God! He's okay.

Hastening on, she parked behind his pickup truck. Her heart raced as she got out and ran to him, shouting, "Brian, Brian, what are you doing? Where are you going? What's wrong?"

He greeted her with an angry look of surprise. "What are you doing here?" he snarled, pushing her away. "Get out of here and leave me alone. I'm going away."

39

"Where are you going?" she screamed. "I don't understand. What's wrong with you?" She charged him again, clinging to his arm.

"Go home!" He pushed her away again.

"No, I won't, and I won't let you go," she cried, grabbing his arm again. "I love you. I know you're upset about the war; I know it's stirred up memories about Vietnam."

"I told you to keep out of that," he shouted. "It's my business."

"It's my business, too. I love you, Brian, don't you understand that? I won't let you go."

"You can't stop me. Now get out of my way!"

She kept her grip on him, and they struggled on the sidewalk in the light of the streetlamp. The loud shouting drew the attention of neighbors, many of whom came out onto their porches to watch or peered outside from behind curtained windows.

Brian broke free. Pushing her aside, he ran to his pickup. Kathy followed him.

"I know it's Vietnam," she screamed. "I know it is. It's been eating at you ever since you came home. You've got to admit it."

"Leave me alone!" he shouted, opening the truck door. He had one leg in when she caught him from behind and grabbed hold of his sleeve.

"Tell me about the Death Ray," she screamed, a flood of tears rolling over her swollen cheeks. She pulled him back around from the open door. "The Death Ray, the Short-timer—what do they mean? Tell me!"

"No! No!" He raised his fist in angry surprise, but stopped short of striking her. "No, no, I can't. I just can't!" He pushed her down onto the sidewalk. "Just go and leave me alone! Leave me alone!"

He started back into his truck when two neighborhood men came running. The bigger of the two hollered at Brian as the other helped Kathy up from the cold sidewalk.

"Maybe you'd like to try pushing me around, buddy," the man said, putting a strong hand on Brian's shoulder. Enraged, Brian quickly turned and pointed his .45 straight into the good Samaritan's face. Turning pale, the man backed away, almost tripping.

40

"Oh my God!" Kathy screamed.

With tear-filled eyes, Brian turned the gun on himself, pointing it to his temple. "Maybe you'd like me to do it right here!" he shouted.

Speechless and shaken, the men retreated trying to drag Kathy with them.

"Oh God, no, Brian," she screamed hysterically. "Don't, don't do it! Please, please … !" Sobbing in despair, she dropped to the ground.

Brian stuffed his handgun into his field jacket pocket, jumped into his pickup, and screeched away, leaving an acrid cloud of burned rubber in his wake.

CHAPTER 7

After Brian Scott left, some of his neighbors came out of their homes and gathered in the street and sidewalk by his apartment. Some quickly went to the aid of the man Brian had threatened.

"He put that gun right in my face," the terrified man gasped, as they helped him to sit down on the curb. "I thought he was going to kill me … I thought he was going to kill me," he repeated.

Kathy, on the other hand, quickly recovered. She focused her thoughts and concerns on Brian alone. To keep him from killing himself, she knew she had to act fast. Ignoring the neighbors and their questions, she ran to Brian's apartment and let herself in. The place smelled of beer. Empty cans littered the living room floor. The TV was on, still tuned to CNN, which continued with its ominous war coverage. She went straight to the phone and dialed 911. Excitedly, she related the episode to the operator, who advised her to calm down and wait for a patrol car that would be there soon.

She banged the receiver down and picked it up again, quickly dialing Arthur and Julie's number. "Please be home, please be home!" she whispered, impatiently. When the answering machine prompted her to leave a message, she quickly said, "There's a problem! Please call me immediately at Brian's." She left the number and hung up, hoping that they would call right back. Pacing nervously, however, she soon gave up waiting and went outside.

"I'm sorry for what happened," she apologized to the small crowd that had formed. "Brian's not well. It's a long story. I've called the police and they should be here any minute."

She grabbed her handbag from her car and raced back into the apartment. She took her wallet from her bag and searched for Arthur Benedict's business card.

"God have mercy." She found Arthur's card and quickly dialed his pager, then entered Brian's apartment phone number.

Going into the front room, she switched off the TV, then quickly returned to the phone and called Brian's father. In a moment, she explained to him all that had happened and the crisis at hand.

"God damn you!" he exploded. "You had no right meddling and bringing up things that are best left alone. If anything happens to my son, I'm blaming you. Do you hear me, you meddling bitch?"

Surprised and crushed by his heartless criticism—and now her own misgivings—she dropped the phone and sunk to the floor in tears. A painful spasm knotted her stomach, and shot up like lightning through her chest, neck and jaw.

"Dear God Almighty," she pleaded in her tears, "please don't let anything happen to him. Please, please don't let anything happen to him."

At a sudden loud knock at the door, Kathy turned to see two police officers on the porch peering in at her on the floor. Not waiting for an invitation, the two came in. The female officer helped Kathy up, and soon had her seated on the sofa, answering questions as calmly as she could.

"He's going to kill himself," she said, as the male officer took notes and joined in the questioning.

"Did he give any indication where he was going?" the woman asked.

"No," Kathy cried, shaking her head. "He didn't say."

It didn't take them much longer to get all the details. Police throughout the city and across New Castle County were quickly alerted to what had happened: *41-year-old Brian Scott, a decorated and despondent Vietnam War veteran, has fled his home in Wilmington's west side after an altercation with his girlfriend.*

Subject threatened a neighbor with a handgun, perhaps a .45 semi-automatic. Subject is suicidal, armed, and considered dangerous.

The Delaware Motor Vehicle Department provided the police with a description of Brian's truck and its license plate number. Kathy described Brian and showed them the photograph on the end table.

"Now we wait," the female officer said. "As soon as he's spotted, we'll pick him up. Most of the time this type of incident turns out all right."

Kathy nodded. "Just don't hurt him. Please don't hurt him. He's a good man."

"I'm sure he is," the male officer said sympathetically. As two additional police cars arrived, he stepped outside to talk with neighbors.

. . .

Brian Scott trembled as he drove up Wilmington's Martin Luther King Boulevard, drowning in the murky depths of depression. He was heading for his welding shop and felt certain no one would be around. When a fine rain began to fall, he switched on his wipers. Then, on coming to the Market Street intersection, he suddenly changed his plan and made a quick left onto the city's main thoroughfare. It was 6:35 p.m. on Saturday, and traffic was nearly non-existent.

A neon sign on Second Street caught his attention. He pulled into an off-street parking area across from it. The lot ran parallel to Second Street, and was nearly empty. Directly across from him, the vintage 1950s sign beckoned one and all to McGuiggan's Pub. He parked, and seeing no one around, he switched off his truck, and doused the lights. The .45 semi-automatic in his jacket pocket pressed against his leg. He pulled the gun out and held it in his lap. A lone car was parked in front of the bar, on the street, yet not a single pedestrian was in sight. The bright headlights of two cars came suddenly into view. Side-by-side, they drag-raced past the bar and quickly disappeared up Second Street. In their wake, the quiet stillness of the night returned.

This is it, he thought, staring blankly at the bar. *This is the spot!* He rested his head wearily on the steering wheel, trying to quell his rampaging mind. "Do it, man!" the voice repeated. "Do it! You owe it to him."

He raised the .45 to his head, struggling to summon the inner strength to do what he had set out to do. But his finger froze on the trigger, and the minutes ticked by. Then it hit him with full force, and he realized where he could find the strength. He tucked the .45 back into his pocket. *I need a drink!*

. . .

At a time when most others had declined, McGuiggan's Pub was one of a handful of bars that continued to have a night life in downtown Wilmington. Known for its blue-collar ambiance, good food, and cold beer, it was a family-run landmark founded by rough and tumble Irishman, John McGuiggan, in 1944. The pub occupied a two-story, brick building on one-way Second Street, near the foot of busy Market Street. The area around it had gone from good to bad, to worse, and back to good again, thanks to the city's never ending urban renewal projects. But somehow, old-time McGuiggan's Pub remained untouched by the renewal and retained its original warmth and charm. In short, it was a colorful vestige of a bygone era.

A gust of cold, wet wind hit Brian as he got out of his pickup. Turning away from it, he pulled up the collar of his field jacket, then crossed the street to the bar. Pausing at the front step to compose himself a bit, he pushed the weighty wooden door open and went in. A man in a black leather jacket and two women in raincoats passed him on their way out. The smell of alcohol and cigarette smoke clung to them.

On the left, at the long bar, Mark Reader and Cheryl Mensinger, regulars at the pub and both in their mid-twenties, sat on swivel stools close to the door, drinking beer and talking with Paddy McGuiggan, the owner and bartender. An overhead TV was tuned to a college basketball game. The room was longer than it was wide, and there were no other patrons at the bar or at the column of tables arranged between the narrow walkway by the bar and the wall.

Paddy and his two customers looked at Brian as he went past them, and couldn't help noticing his ashen, disheveled appearance.

"Welcome to McGuiggan's," Paddy called.

"Hey," Brian muttered, with his head down. He walked over the worn, wood planked floor to the end of the room, where he sat facing front, at the very last table. Mark and Cheryl turned to one another and exchanged anxious looks.

"Whoa," Mark said, "wonder what's ailin' that guy?"

His girlfriend nodded. "Looks like he just saw a ghost or lost his last best friend." She picked up her glass of beer and took a drink. Then she lit a cigarette and took a long drag.

With a grin, Paddy turned from the couple, threw his hand towel over his shoulder, and walked the length of the bar to wait on his customer.

"Still raining out?" the heavy-set man asked as he approached Brian. Brian just stared at the tabletop and didn't reply.

Paddy's smile vanished. "What can I get you?" he said, more abruptly.

Brian looked up. "Shot of bourbon and a draft chaser."

"Any particular brand?"

"Nope."

"Ok, comin' right up," the bartender said. "Like to see a menu? The regular cook won't be in until a little later when things pick up, but I can fix you up if you're hungry."

"Nah," Brian said, with a shake of his head.

In no time, Paddy returned with the drinks and set them on the table in front of him. "There you go. Enjoy!"

Brian muttered something inaudible as he picked up the shot glass.

Paddy turned to leave but stopped. He had a funny feeling about this customer. He watched him down the bourbon, then he asked, "Pardon me for asking, buddy, but are you okay?"

Brian wiped a hand across his mouth and set the shot glass down on the table. "Yeah," he said, with an odd grin, "My strength's returning already."

Paddy nodded, not knowing what to make of the comment. On the way back behind the bar, he said, "Just give me a holler if you need anything else."

Looking over the room, Brian took a drink of beer. The volume on the TV was low enough as not to be intrusive. Brian felt his .45 through his jacket. *One more round and I'm out of here*, he thought, already feeling the heat of the booze, and gaining the courage to quiet that inner voice.

. . .

Back in Brian's apartment, Kathy jumped up from the sofa when the telephone suddenly rang. "Brian?" she shouted hopefully into the receiver. "

"No, it's Doctor Benedict. You called my pager. Kathy? Is this you?"

"Yes, oh, Arthur, thank God it's you," she said, fast and frantic. "Something horrible has happened. Brian has a gun and he's going to hurt himself. The police are searching for him. It's all so crazy, like a terrible nightmare. I'm so worried! I don't know what to do."

"Calm down, Kathy, you're going too fast. Try to calm yourself. Now, where are you?"

"I'm at Brian's apartment in Wilmington. The police are here with me."

"Give me the address and we'll leave right away. It'll take a few minutes. Julie and I are at a restaurant just across the state line in Pennsylvania. When your number came through on my pager, I didn't recognize it. Sorry I didn't call back right away."

"It's all right. Just come as quickly as you can." She gave him the address and moments later, the Benedicts were speeding south on Route 202, toward the Delaware state line and the nearby city of Wilmington.

. . .

Shortly after 7:00 p.m., on their normal rounds, two police officers cruised up Second Street in their patrol car, going past McGuiggan's. One of the officers happened to spot a pickup truck that matched the recently dispatched description of Brian Scott's vehicle. The officers turned onto Market Street and then quickly turned into the little parking area, where they stopped behind the suspicious truck. The license plate checked out. They had found Brian's truck and quickly relayed the information to headquarters. Meanwhile, they returned to Market Street and parked out of the way, to keep an inconspicuous eye on the truck.

. . .

Inside the bar, Paddy returned to Brian's table. "Another round?"

Brian sat with his head down and his hands cupped around his empty glass of beer. Paddy rapped his knuckles on the table. "Yo, another round?" he repeated.

Startled, Brian looked up. "Yeah!" He handed Paddy his glass, while the bartender picked up the shot glass.

"Be right back."

When Paddy returned with the drinks, Brian quickly downed the shot of bourbon, as Paddy went back behind the bar.

"Hey, Paddy," Mark said. "How about switching off this one-sided game and put the news on. Before we came in, we heard that the ground war had started. Our troops are on the move."

"Is that right?" Paddy said, looking surprised while surfing through the channels for CNN.

Overhearing, Brian looked up. Suddenly, he was listening intently.

Mark glanced at his girlfriend. "Yeah. Hey, did you know Cheryl's brother is over there?"

"No, I didn't," Paddy said, his round face lighting with surprise. "What outfit is he with?" he asked, finally landing on CNN.

"The 82nd Airborne," Cheryl said, looking up with a shake of her long auburn hair.

"You don't say!"

Cheryl nodded. "Afraid so. He signed up not long after getting out of high school. It was something he wanted to do."

"How long's he been in?"

"Almost four years," Mark said. "Right, Cheryl?"

Nodding, she said, "It'll be four years next month, and his hitch will be up. My mom and dad were praying the ground war wouldn't start until after that. We were all praying. In a month, he'd be home, safe and sound."

Mark put his arm around her and pulled her close. "He'll be fine," he assured.

"Only a month to go!" Paddy mused. "Hell, he's a short-timer. Too short for combat. But I wouldn't worry about it, Cheryl. This war's gonna be a cake walk. It'll be over in a blink of an eye. Betcha!"

"I hope you're right," she replied.

Listening, Brian teared up again. He got up and went into the Men's Room at the back of the pub. On the television, a CNN commentator announced that allied ground forces were moving en masse, and that the long-anticipated ground offensive had finally begun. Meanwhile, across Second Street from McGuiggan's, near Brian's truck, additional police had arrived, and a search of the area was started. The sergeant on the scene sent two officers to check the pub, and others to canvass the nearby bus terminal and Amtrak railway station.

"Look for a guy in jeans and an O. D. green, Army field jacket," the sergeant said. "That's what he was wearing."

CHAPTER 8

McGuiggan's heavy front door creaked open, letting a gust of cold air inside. Surprised by the sudden chill, Mark and Cheryl turned to see two police officers come in and shake water off their heavy rain gear. Paddy immediately recognized the two men, who stayed by the door, giving the room a visual once over. It was not unusual for the police to come in now and then just to check on things, so Paddy knew quite a few of the men and women on the force. In addition, many liked to frequent the bar during their off-duty hours.

"Hey, Paddy," the taller officer said, stepping over to the bar. "How's it going?" His partner remained motionless and stoic by the door.

Paddy smiled. "Quiet night for now, fellas. Everything's fine."

"Good to hear," the officer replied. "We're making rounds and thought we'd stop in to make sure things are A-okay in Wilmington's hottest hot spot."

Paddy laughed. "Some hot spot!"

Turning serious, the policeman continued. "Say, you haven't seen anything of a forty-one-year-old white male, medium build, dirty blond hair, wearing jeans and an Army field jacket?"

Paddy's cordial smile vanished, replaced by a look of shocked surprise. Mark and Cheryl swiveled around to see Brian step back into the room. With all eyes riveted on him, he froze, and for the next few moments, no one moved or said a word. Finally, the cop by the bar spoke up. "Brian Scott?"

Brian pulled his handgun and pointed it straight at the stunned officer. "Get out of here," he shouted, stepping forward. "Leave me alone! Get out! Get out! I'm not going anywhere with you."

Paddy, Mark and Cheryl remained stone still as the cop took cautious steps backward, moving toward his partner by the door.

"Take it easy, buddy," he said. "Take it easy. We're leaving."

"Go on—get the hell outta here," Brian demanded. "Get out!" His eyes were red and swollen from crying.

. . .

Across town, in Stanton, Brian's father paced the floor of his mobile home. He crushed out a cigarette in a butt-filled ashtray and quickly lit another.

"Damn that woman," he cursed aloud, still furious with Kathy Hamilton for precipitating the crisis with Brian. In the kitchen, he dropped two ice cubes into a glass, then poured whiskey and a little water over them. The booze went down real easy, and it helped to ease his anger.

He thought about his son, painfully recalling that night so long ago. *I had been drinking then too. The night I ruined my relationship with Brian. God, how I wish I could go back and change things!*

He sipped his drink, and let the potent whiskey sit in his mouth for a moment, savoring it before swallowing. Drinking had always been a friend to him, comforting and easing so many painful memories, especially those of the hellish days and nights in the Pacific, in places with names rarely mentioned any longer except by old veterans like himself.

Helen! He thought of his late wife. *Oh God, how I miss her. She was so lovely, my best—maybe only—friend!* He envisioned her the way she was before Brian's year in Vietnam sparked a God-awful depression that turned her into a sickly, morose version of her former self. *A victim of her own worry and anxiety. Relentlessly tormented ... and never recovering.* Welling up with emotion, he took another drink. *Her name should be on that damned wall in Washington, too.*

"Damn that war!" he snarled, gazing into his drink as the past seemed to become the present and Helen was there with him in the kitchen. He drank more whiskey and blew more cigarette smoke across the portals of time and memory to hear his very own voice, albeit younger and more robust, berating his beloved son and the others who served in Vietnam.

"I'm tellin' you, Helen, they're a bunch of whining crybabies. They didn't have it so bad, not like we did. One year and they were out. We were in for the duration, or we came home in a box—or worse, crippled."

Of course she protested the cruel, unjustified characterization, but in his stubborn pride and arrogance, he ignored her. While arguing, he didn't hear Brian come home, nor did he realize he had heard his booze-charged tirade, until it was too late.

Oh God, you know how many times I have prayed that I could take back those words. Too many to count, and all in vain.

In his anger and self-disappointment, he threw his drink against the wall, trying to shatter the memory, but only succeeding in sending a hail of glass, booze, and ice through the kitchen. Turning away, he went into his bedroom and, kneeling on arthritic knees, looked beneath his bed for the old family album. Finding it, he blew dust off the thick book and sat down on the bed to scan the many photographs within its pages. Each photo brought back a special memory from long ago, of Helen, his beautiful Helen of Troy, and of his precious Brian, as a youngster and later, a man in uniform.

"Brian ... Brian ... Brian," he muttered, staring through tears, fondly caressing each photo, each memory, in his wounded heart. *My only child, my living link to the past, and my hope for the future. Brian ... Brian ...*

Finally, he set the book aside and picked up the phone on the nightstand to make an urgent call. "This is Brian Scott, Sr.," he said to the police sergeant. "You are searching for my son. I want to help."

. . .

The moment the two police officers backed out of the pub, Brian turned his .45 on Paddy, ordering him to come over the bar and lock the front door. Standing out of the way, Mark and Cheryl watched. They were much too frightened to move or say a word.

"Turn out the sign and those front lights," Brian ordered. "And pull the blinds."

Paddy didn't hesitate. He switched them off, and lowered the blinds, rendering the room dim and somber.

"Is your back door locked?"

"Yeah," Paddy said, with a nod. "I always keep it locked. Hey, if you want money, you can have whatever's in the register and get out the back. If you stay, the police will surround the place and get you for sure." He hoped Brian would listen to reason and follow his suggestion.

Mark and Cheryl were too numb to move. They prayed that he would leave quickly. Yet, for Brian, the sudden development only bolstered his resolve to carry out his misguided plan, and the voice within him became more insistent that he do so.

"I don't want your money," Brian finally said, in a halting voice. "I don't want anything. I'm not going to hurt anyone. I didn't come in here to do that." He pointed the .45 at the television, demanding, "Turn that damn thing off!"

Paddy walked cautiously past him and around the bar, where he quickly found the remote and switched off the TV. The abrupt silence made the atmosphere acutely more unnerving.

Somehow, Paddy mustered the courage to ask, "If you don't want money, then why did you come in here?" His words seemed to echo off the silent walls.

Keeping the .45 pointed at them, Brian ran a hand across his forehead, back and forth, as if to relieve a headache.

"I came in to get ripped!" he declared angrily. "To get drunk enough to find the courage to end my sorry-ass, miserable life. That's why!"

Thunderstruck, they looked at him with disbelief. His blunt admission upset them even more. Cheryl put her hands over her face and cried. Her sobbing reverberated through the room.

"Shhh," Mark cautioned, pulling her close. "Quiet." He was afraid she might push him into using his gun. But the young woman wouldn't be consoled or silenced.

"Why?" she asked, noting the tears in Brian's eyes. "Why would you want to do such a terrible thing?"

"That's my business," he snapped. But on seeing her so distraught with concern, he momentarily thought of Kathy.

"You're going to kill yourself in here?" Paddy asked, in surprise.

"No, I mean, I will, but I didn't plan to. Not here."

"Well," said Paddy, pointing to the back of the bar, "unless you get out while you still have the chance, you're going to be trapped in here."

"It's too late," Brian said. "I'm staying right here." He fell silent, then said, "I have to think. Just let me think." He paused again before adding, "We're stuck with each other. I didn't want it this way." Brian put a hand to his sweaty forehead, thinking and trying to settle his racing mind.

"Why don't you just let us all go out the front?" Paddy asked. "You can stay."

Brian thought about that, then said, "No, no one's leaving."

"If no one's leaving," Paddy continued, trying to keep him talking, "what do you want us to do? Sit here?"

Brian did not reply. His inner voice was speaking to him, urging him to hurry. *Do it, man! Do it!*

Finally, when the voice subsided, he said to them, "Just let me think. Let me think!"

In his mind's eye, he saw Kathy, crying and flailing her arms at him, pleading with him outside his apartment, "Tell me what's wrong! Tell me about the Death Ray—the Death Ray and the Short-timer! Tell me!" The vision was such a bitter one, he collapsed into a chair, weeping.

"Leave the poor guy alone," Mark cautioned Paddy. "Just let him be."

The captives watched intently as he sobbed, each wondering what could be responsible for such a profound emotional breakdown. They understood the danger they were in, yet they could only feel compassion for this stranger that was threatening them. No one wanted to see him harmed.

When Brian finally calmed, he got up and paced the floor. Stopping, he looked at Cheryl and said, "I hope your brother comes home from the war okay. I said a prayer for him while I was sitting back there drinking. I prayed for them all—even the Iraqis." He paused thoughtfully before adding, "I wish someone could find a way to put an end to war. If I had the opportunity, I'd grab it by the neck and put a round right through its skull. I'd rid the world of that son-of-a-bitch once and for all. I would!"

After another pause, and despite Mark's warning, Paddy spoke up again, "With us in here and the police outside," he said, "I'm figuring it's going to be a long night. Why don't we all sit down? Maybe we could talk a little? Maybe you'd tell us what's wrong, why you want to do what you said? It couldn't hurt. What do you say?"

All eyes were on Brian, wondering how he would react to such a direct suggestion.

"No, no!" he snapped. "It won't make any difference. It's too late; it's too late for anything."

Another long, unnerving pause followed. All eyes were focused on Brian as they wondered what his next move would be.

Cheryl felt certain that Paddy had tried to get him engaged and talking solely to relieve the terrible tension and put off an imminent disaster. Taking a gamble, she pushed the attempt a bit further with a little levity.

"Well, I don't know about the rest of you," she said, matter-of-factly, "but I could really go for a beer. Why don't we all sit and have a cold one?"

After thinking on it, Brian nodded at Mark, telling him, "Push a couple of these tables together. And you, bartender, get me another bourbon and fill a couple pitchers with beer, and bring 'em over."

Mark went straight to work, and Cheryl moved chairs in place around the two tables, then she helped Paddy with the glasses.

When everything was arranged, Brian moved to the head of the table, facing the front door. He pointed to the others to sit. Mark and Cheryl sat at his left, and Paddy at his right, closest to the bar.

"Like the last supper," Brian noted dryly, looking over the adjoined tables at the others. With his .45, he pointed to the glasses by the pitchers and said, "Everyone take a glass, and, Bartender, start pouring."

They each picked up a glass and Paddy filled them with beer. He poured one for Brian too and passed it to him.

Brian downed the shot of bourbon, then raised his glass of beer chaser as if to make a toast. "Drink up," he said. "Misery likes company." Brian and the others all took a drink of beer.

"Now what?" Paddy asked, setting his glass down, wondering what was coming next.

With all eyes fixed on Brian, he sat down, the .45 still in his tight grip. "Now," he said, with a look of sadness, "I've decided ... I'm going to tell you something I've never told anyone. It's the story of the Short-timer, and it's one miserable, damn story."

. . .

After leaving the restaurant, Arthur and Julie Benedict practically ran to their car, and in no time, they were speeding south on Pennsylvania Route 202, heading back to Delaware. They made excellent time until crossing the state line and reaching the Concord Pike section of the highway, where the choking sprawl of commercial development led to traffic congestion and a much slower pace. At the Fairfax Shopping Center, Arthur steered his sporty BMW west, away from the congestion and onto the more rural Route 141, where he quickly picked up speed again. Julie glanced worriedly at the speedometer.

"Arthur," she cautioned, "you'd better slow down. You're doing seventy."

Arthur decelerated slightly. "I know," he said. "I know. But we'll be there shortly."

Julie focused on the road ahead, illuminated by the car's bright high beams. Arthur kept the radio tuned to a Philadelphia FM station devoted solely to classical music. Debussy's *Clair de Lune* played softly in the background. Its beautiful, lilting melody of moonlight rendered the atmosphere in the car calm and peaceful. Yet, as calming as it was, it had little effect on allaying their fears and apprehensions. When the music ended, Julie asked, "Do you think he'll do it?"

Arthur shrugged. "I hope not, but he's got a gun, and he's obviously depressed, probably with PTSD." He paused, then added grimly, "I'm afraid it's highly possible."

Trying to digest that straight up pessimism, Julie paused, then muttered, "Poor Kathy. She must be out of her mind with worry."

Arthur nodded. "I only hope we're not too late. The mind is complex and complicated, but we're learning more and more about it every day. Perhaps someday ...." His voice broke off, leaving the thought unfinished and giving free reign to a soft concerto coming from the radio.

. . .

At Brian's apartment, the police officers had been notified that the missing man had been located at a downtown bar. They were instructed to inform Kathy Hamilton of the situation and to ask her if she would be willing to come to the scene.

"Of course I'll go," she readily agreed. "Just try to stop me!"

Minutes later, as she sat in the back of a police car, waiting to be taken downtown, Arthur and Julie pulled up in their car. Arthur flashed his lights and parked. When Kathy spotted them, she jumped out of the police car.

"Thank God you're here," she said, hugging Julie. Arthur moved close and threw his arms around the two of them, hugging them both.

"Are you okay, Kathy?" Arthur asked.

"Yes," she replied, wiping tears from her eyes. "They've found him! He's in a bar on Second Street."

A police car pulled up next to them. Through the open window, the driver said, "We've got to go, Miss Hamilton! There's no time to waste."

Kathy pulled away from the Benedicts, and replied to the officer "Okay, I'm ready."

"We'll go with you!" Julie said.

Kathy quickly explained to the policeman. "This is Dr. Arthur Benedict, Chief Psychologist at the Veterans Hospital, and his wife, Julie, is an RN there. Can they go with me? They would be very helpful."

The officer nodded. "Okay, that's fine, but hurry and get in."

The three got in immediately and, with lights flashing, the driver sped off, heading downtown for McGuiggan's Pub.

CHAPTER 9

Paddy McGuiggan squirmed uncomfortably in his seat at the table. "Would you mind lowering that gun," he politely asked Brian. "It's pointing right at me and making me a little nervous." He nodded toward the .45 in Brian's hand on the tabletop.

Complying, Brian turned the muzzle toward the wall. He took another drink of beer, then sucked in a deep breath and said, "I've gotta be half-tanked to tell you this. Like I said, I've kept it locked inside and never spoke about it. I sure couldn't tell it to my father. But before I check out, after so many years, I'm going to tell you three because ... because someone ought to know. This thing has been hanging 'round my neck for twenty-three years, since 1968 when I was just a nineteen-year-old kid."

Paddy, Mark, and Cheryl sat in full attention, with their eyes riveted on him, wondering what awful thing he was going to tell them. *What could he have done to push him to such a drastic decision?*

Brian took another drink of beer. "1968," he began, "was a bad year for a lot of people. The Vietnam War was going hot and heavy and, like a lot of guys, I had been drafted into the Army. I had a girlfriend back home, but by the time I returned, she was married and had a baby on the way. She seemed happy.

"My father never told me in so many words, but I know he believes that the war killed my mom. I think he thought that her constant worrying about me threw her into some deep depression she never climbed out of. It killed his spirit when she died. He's never been the same. My father went through hell in the Pacific fighting the Japanese during the Second World War. He was quite a man. He doesn't think too much of 'Nam vets, though."

Choked with painful emotion, Brian paused and turned away from his listeners. When he looked back, they noticed that his eyes had teared up once again.

"Anyway," he resumed, "what I'm going to tell you is not about my father or war veterans or anything else. It's about me and the Death Ray. It's the story of the Short-timer."

The listeners exchanged glances of confusion.

"The Short-timer," said Cheryl. "That's what Paddy said they call soldiers with just a little time left to serve—soldiers like my brother. Is that what your story is about?"

"Yes," Brian said.

Suddenly, the phone behind the bar rang, startling everyone, especially Brian, who quickly jumped out of his seat, pointing his .45 at the entrance door and causing the others to duck their heads onto the tabletop. The ringing continued.

"Should I answer it?" Paddy said, recovering.

With a nod from Brian, the big man climbed over the bar and picked up the phone. "McGuiggan's Pub," he gasped, breathing heavily from the sudden exertion. "Yeah ... Paddy McGuiggan, the owner. Yes, everyone's fine, Officer. He's telling a story about Vietnam. I don't know. I'll ask him." Paddy set the receiver on his shoulder and said to Brian, "It's the police. They'd like to talk with you."

Brian shook his head. "When I'm finished, then I'll talk with them."

Paddy spoke to the officer. "Did you hear that? He says when he's finished, he'll talk to you. I have no idea how long it'll take."

Irritated, Brian shouted, "Hang up!"

Paddy cut off the conversation immediately and hung up.

"Put the phone on the bar and come back with us."

As instructed, Paddy set the phone on the bar top, then climbed back over the bar and returned to his chair.

"When I'm finished," Brian told them, "you can all leave. You'll be free to go."

"You mean you're going to just let us go?" asked Mark in surprise.

"Yes. As soon as I'm finished—everyone can di-di outta here."

On emphasizing that point, welcome relief flashed over each of the listeners' faces. Brian raised his glass and motioned for them to do the same. Looking at Cheryl, he said, "To your brother in the 82nd and to all our troops, especially the short-timers." With that, he emptied his glass. The others did, too.

Brian passed his glass to Paddy. "It's going to be your job to see that no one's glass goes empty for long."

Paddy smiled. "No problem. I can handle it."

Mark suddenly spoke up, asking, "Is it a long story?"

"No—it's a miserable story."

. . .

After arriving on the scene, Captain Francis "Frank" Rutkowski of the Wilmington Police Department, promptly chewed out the young sergeant for sending two patrolmen into McGuiggan's to "royally screw things up." Rutkowski set up his command post on lower Market Street. He deployed his cops around the bar and had them cordon off the streets around it.

"Thank God it's Saturday night." Rutkowski said, trying to find a bright spot. "If this were a weeknight, we'd be up to our necks in work traffic."

Rutkowski was a gruff, old-school, up-through-the-ranks policeman, well respected by both ordinary cops and city officials for his abilities and experience that spanned a career of over twenty-four years on the force. He rarely cursed, but when he did it was usually during trying times of great anger and disappointment.

"If those guys would have used their heads and telephoned McGuiggan's before waltzing in there," Rutkowski barked to his assistant, Lieutenant John Manly, "maybe McGuiggan could have warned his customers and they could have gotten out. Now we're dealing with a damn suicide-hostage situation."

61

Experience had taught the captain that even the most routine situations can quickly become disasters if mismanaged. "That's the Rutkowski Principle," he'd tell anyone who cared to listen. "And it's our job to see that it doesn't happen. That's what they pay us to do."

Rutkowski gazed down deserted Market Street toward McGuiggan's. "I'm getting too old for this stuff, John," he complained to Manly.

"Yes, sir," the ramrod straight, six-foot, black officer replied.

"What's the story on this guy?"

Manly was quick to reply. "Name's Brian Scott—41-year-old white male, Vietnam veteran, who operates a welding service not too far from here off MLK Boulevard. According to his girlfriend, Kathy Hamilton, he's distraught and depressed over something that might have happened to him during his Vietnam service. Our guys are currently bringing her here and she should arrive any minute."

"Any history of mental problems?"

"None that we know of."

"Police record?"

"No, he's clean. Can't even find a traffic violation on him. In fact, he won the Bronze Star for bravery in Vietnam. Sounds like a model citizen. It just doesn't seem right."

Rutkowski adjusted his service cap and watched the light rain fall by the streetlamp at Second and Market. "There's a whole lot about life that's not right, John. The older I get, the clearer that becomes."

Manly nodded. "I hear you, Captain."

"Well, now that this thing has turned into a standoff, I suppose we're going to have to call in Patton and the Third Army."

"SWAT?"

"Yeah, but if I have any trouble with Russ—" He left the thought unfinished and shook his head.

Russ was Lieutenant Russell Vinton, leader of the Department's eighteen-man SWAT force, and known for his bravado, hard-drinking, and contempt of protocol.

"He's controversial, all right," Manly said. "A little too intense."

62

Rutkowski laughed. "That's a fine way to put it, John," He patted his friend on the shoulder. "You're going to go far in this modern force of the nineties. In addition to SWAT, let's get our negotiations team out here and see if we can't locate someone from inspections or an employee who might be able to describe the physical layout of the building."

Lieutenant Manly interrupted. "We've got plenty of people right here who've been known to frequent McGuiggan's."

"I know, and I've spent a few nights in there myself. But if we're forced to go in, we'll need someone who's familiar with the entire layout—the kitchen, the basement, and the upstairs. The whole place."

"I'll get right on it, Captain. Anything else?"

"Yeah, let's get our mobile office here so we can get out of this rain. It looks like we're going to be here for a while."

Manly nodded.

"And let me know the moment Scott's girlfriend shows up. She might be the key to a peaceful resolution—oh, and be sure to keep the media dogs in their cage." Rutkowski paused and put a hand to his head. "I've got a headache and a half! You wouldn't happen to have any aspirin?"

Manly shrugged. "Sorry, I don't, but I'll ask around."

CHAPTER 10

"Vietnam!" Brian Scott said, morosely, leaning forward in his chair and recalling the little southeast Asian country he couldn't have found on a map before 1968. "That damn place changed me forever, and it ripped the heart and soul out of my family and country. I wish to God I had never gone there."

He tapped a hand nervously against the tabletop, while keeping a tight grip on the .45 with the other.

"The 'Nam," he muttered, "the asshole of the world, the Army's piss tube, Asia's arm pit—the grunts had a million names for it, none of 'em good. 'Grunts' and 'ground-pounders' are what they called us infantry guys, like in grunting, ground-pounding, pack animals."

He raised his glass and took another drink of beer, remembering.

"Vietnam brings up many different images to people," he continued, "but for me it'll always mean senseless death and destruction, and a constant reminder of failure—especially my failure."

Stopping again, he emptied his glass, and then turned to Paddy for a refill, which came immediately.

"I got there in June of 1968, and it still feels like just yesterday. I was part of a plane load of replacements, soldiers from the states, mostly grunts. We wore spanking new jungle fatigues and boots. So, we really stood out on our arrival at the military base at Da Nang. Right after we got off the plane, the base was hit with a rocket attack, and we took cover like all the rest. Later, they told us it was our official welcome to 'Nam. Yeah, that's how they put it. Some welcome. Couple of guys were killed.

"Our real welcome was the heat and humidity. They hit us like a one-two punch the moment we got off the air-conditioned plane. I found out in spades how they could drain even the toughest soldier. It was no joke, and took some getting used to. I'll never forget it. I was sweating bullets for a solid year, but we managed."

As Brian spoke, the others noticed he seemed to regain some steadiness in his composure. He didn't appear so scattered and frantic. *At least*, they thought, *he's not talking about killing himself.* And unbeknownst to one another, they wanted to keep things that way by questioning him.

Paddy was the first to speak up, asking, "Did you stay at DaNang?"

"No," Brian replied. "The next day, I boarded a C-130 and flew south to Chu Lai, another huge military base that stretched along the South China Sea." He glanced at Paddy. "You'll like this, bartender. Inside the base, I once saw a field of beer. It was half the size of a football field and filled with pallets stacked high with beer cans. I couldn't believe it.

"I reported to the reception center there and stayed for a couple of days, sitting through classes designed to teach us what it would take a lifetime to learn about that country."

Cheryl spoke up to ask a question. "How about the language? Did they teach you guys how to speak to the people over there?"

Brian shook his head. "No, that would have taken too long. They taught us just a few words and phrases. *Dung lai* was one. It meant, Stop! When we yelled it at the enemy or suspected enemy, they knew they had better stop running or risk getting shot. *Di-di mau* was another, it meant to hurry up. *Boom-boom* was another. It was slang, and if you think about it, you can figure out its meaning. It didn't take us long.

"As new soldiers in-country, we had to write our names on the insides of both of our jungle boots."

"Inside your boots?" Mark interrupted. "What was that about?"

"Identification," Brian said, glancing back at him. "In case you had your legs blown off, they could figure out which leg belonged to which body. And it happened … too often."

Brian paused, then continued. "As a new guy in-country," he said, "I had a lot of paperwork to fill out—legal stuff. One damn form after another, from financial stuff to insurance. When our indoctrination ended, it was time to start earning our money, time to start killing people."

Hearing that, the others shifted uneasily in their seats.

"So, they put me and another new guy on a deuce-and-a-half supply truck, and we traveled south of Chu Lai, going on the famous Highway One. We drove for five miles or so to a place called Landing Zone Badger, or LZ Badger for short. It was another base, but just a small outpost, surrounded by a security perimeter of concertina wire and sandbagged bunkers. It was the base camp of our new outfit. The other guy with me was Mexican-American and came from New York. Raul Arano was his name. He spoke with an accent, and we had become close friends. I called him *Amigo*.

"Highway One was no highway at all. It was nothing but a dusty old dirt road, and it gave us our first real look at things. Water buffaloes, Vietnamese soldiers on little whiney motorcycles, people walking with all sorts of heavy loads balanced on their backs or heads, trucks overloaded with people hanging all over them—papasans, mamasans and babysans in conical hats and black pajamas—it was a sight. Everything was covered with brown dust from the dirt road, too, stirred up by this stream of miserable traffic. The smell of water buffalo crap made everything even more memorable.

"It was pushing on toward dusk when we rolled through the gate at LZ Badger. Inside the perimeter, we passed sandbagged bunkers and hooches, and the driver soon dropped us directly in front of the hootch that was Bravo Company's headquarters."

Brian abruptly stopped speaking, and his demeanor changed again. Ashen faced, he went quiet in thought. He glanced to Cheryl, to her boyfriend, and finally to Paddy. He raised the .45 off the table and looked it over. Transfixed, the captives watched his every move.

What's wrong? they wondered. *Why the sudden change? What's he thinking about now?* They exchanged anxious glances as the seconds ticked by.

Growing antsy, Paddy took a drink of beer, and was about to speak, when the veteran suddenly asked, "Where was I?" He made no mention of the sudden lapse, and neither did the others.

"The truck driver dropped you at the new base camp." Cheryl quickly reminded him.

"Yeah, that's right," Brian said, remembering. Then, he paused once again to look around the table at each one of them. Finally, he went on with his narrative. From this point forward, he spoke much differently—with such intensity, emotion, and passion that his listeners thought he had somehow, inexplicably, drifted into a state of pseudo reality. He seemed to be re-experiencing his flashback narrative in real time. They found it both weird and fascinating, and they all got emotionally caught up in the realism of his account.

. . .

The hot Vietnamese sun was descending into the western sky when the two replacements got out of the deuce-and-a-half supply truck and thanked the driver.

"Bravo Company, HQ," Brian read the crude hand-painted sign next to the screened door of the sandbagged, wood and canvas hooch. Brian and Raul stood looking over what they thought was going to be their new home for the next twelve months. The driver put the deuce-and-a-half into gear and drove on through the little town of similar hooches, leaving a cloud of dust in his wake.

Raul grinned. "*Hijole*! This doesn't look so bad," he said. "I can do this."

"I hear ya, *Amigo*!" Brian said. "Not too shabby at all."

Two .51 caliber machine guns, on chest-high metal tripods, stood like silent sentinels near the entrance of the hooch. Noticing them, Raul observed, "These ain't American. *Ni hablar!*"

"No," Brian agreed. "Maybe Chi-Com or Russian."

"What do you think they're doin' here?"

Brian shrugged. "Beats me. Maybe they're souvenirs captured from the enemy."

"*Madre mía!*" Raul exclaimed, with a shake of his head. "Must have been some firefight!"

A sergeant heard the men talking outside and opened the screen door. "Yo, you the new guys?" he called out.

"Yes, Sergeant," the two promptly replied.

"I was expecting you a lot earlier," the black Staff Sergeant said. "What held you up?"

"You know the army, Sarge," Brian said. "Hurry up and wait! Delay after delay."

With a smile, the Sergeant nodded. "I've been hurrying up and waiting for over twenty years now. Okay, so get on in here."

Inside the hooch, the sergeant introduced himself. "I'm Sergeant Prescott, the company supply sergeant. Welcome to Bravo Company. Our First Sergeant and Executive Officer are away, so it's just me here right now. The company is out in the bush on an operation. You'll be joining them tomorrow."

Surprised, Raul spoke up, "Hijole! You mean we're not staying here?"

"That'll be a negative," the burly man said, with a half-smile. "You guys are riflemen, grunts, so you'll be choppered out to the unit as soon as possible. The company is understrength as it is."

"Understrength," Brian repeated. "Why's that, Sarge."

With raised eyebrows, Prescott said, "You don't want to know, son."

Brian and Raul exchanged worried glances.

"You guys had chow?" Prescott asked. And on learning they hadn't eaten, he told them to go to the mess hall. "It's just up the road a bit. Big tent, you passed it on your way here. Can't miss it. Just tell 'em I sent you and that you're Bravo replacements. The cook is number one, so it's a chance for one last good meal before your diet turns to C-rations. When you get back, I'll issue you your M-16s and the rest of your combat gear. Now, go on. Di-di!"

The two men walked toward the mess hall.

"One last good meal," Raul mimicked the sergeant. *"Madre mía!"*

"Yeah," Brian shrugged. "I didn't like that sound of that."

When the two left for chow, the plan had been set. Sometime in the morning, a chopper would take them approximately twenty-four klicks northwest, about 15 miles, to a jungle location where Bravo Company had been on a search and destroy mission for weeks. But Army plans, as the two knew, often changed in the blink of an eye, and so it turned out in this case. While they were at the mess hall, Sergeant Prescott received a radio call from the Chu Lai base. It seemed there was a problem with Scott and Arano's paperwork. An orderly had already lost or misplaced some of their documents and they were ordered to return ASAP.

"How we gettin' back to Chu Lai, Sarge?" Scott asked the sergeant, after he broke the news to them.

"Jeep," Prescott said. "We're expecting a resupply chopper back from the bush any minute. It was out dropping off ammo and C-rats for the men. It's bringing back a grunt who has an appointment at the Evac Hospital in Chu Lai in the morning. He has some sort of stomach bug. You can ride along with him. You'll be in good hands, believe me!"

"Ay, caramba!" Raul shrugged. "Back to Chu Lai in the morning."

"Yeah," the Sergeant said with a chuckle. "Count your blessings. Any day out of the bush is a good day."

Prescott went on to issue them their combat gear, including M-16 rifles, ammo and magazines, rucksacks, pistol belts, and web gear with ammo pouches. "They'll give you grenades and claymores, and maybe a couple flares when you get out there."

They were almost finished when the whoop, whoop, whoop sound of an approaching chopper came into earshot.

"Bird comin' in," the Sergeant said. It clattered over the hooch and set down at the nearby landing zone. "That'll be ours," Prescott said. Minutes later, the screen door opened and slammed shut with a crash, startling Brian and Raul, who both turned nervously toward the sound.

"What the hell," Brian said, reacting to the sudden disturbance.

A dirty-faced, muddied grunt had come inside the hooch and stood on the plywood floor by the door, chewing tobacco and staring silently at them. He held a burnt-out looking M-16 and wore a dirty O. D. green bandana around his neck. A bandoleer of M-16 magazines was draped across his chest. The grunt dropped his muddied rucksack onto the floor with a thud, and pulled off his camouflaged, steel-pot helmet.

Holy shit! Brian said to himself, backing up a step. *Who in the hell is this dude?* Following suit, Arano stepped back too. In their pristine jungle fatigues, they felt the sharp sting of intimidation.

The hardened grunt stood about six feet, maybe a little taller, and was lean and muscular like a Special Forces guy. His hair was dark red and worn in a crew cut. His unshaven, leathery face was tanned and freckled, set off by eyebrows nearly bleached white from the sun. His jungle fatigues were torn and tattered, filthy, and stained with white, salty sweat. His sleeves were rolled up to the elbows, exposing two muscular, freckled forearms covered with prominent lettuce-leaf veins. A jagged scar cut an angle above his right eye and another similar scar marred his right cheek. His face was twisted into a mean, angry scowl, clearly indicating he was pissed-off about something. In short, the guy had that look and aura that would send shivers up the back of any man, even Jack the Ripper!

"Jackson!" Sergeant Prescott greeted him with a half-smile. "Glad you made it in okay. Come on in."

The frightful sight glared hard at Prescott, then in a thick Southern drawl, complained, "Glad ya made it in, my ass! I shoulda made it 'in' a damn week ago and stayed in. 'Member, I'm goin' home in a few days. I'm too fuckin' short for this here bullshit!"

Scott and Arano turned nervously to the sergeant, whose smile had vanished.

"I hear what you're saying, Jackson," Prescott said, "and I know you've got a case of the ass. I understand. If it were up to me, I'd hold you back here until you leave for home. Believe me, I would. But it's not up to me! The company commander makes those decisions, and he wants you along for this upcoming operation. I have no say in it! The company's short-handed, remember? I'm sure that's why the Old Man's keeping you in the bush. These two new men are going to help a little on that score."

Jackson didn't buy any of it. He glared at Scott and Arano and spit tobacco juice onto the floor. "Fuckin' bullshit! Lotta good they're doin' me."

Prescott quickly stiffened up. "No need for that," he cautioned. "I can't blame you for being pissed, but there's no need for that."

For a few moments, no one moved or said a word. Then, with a smile, Prescott, changed the subject. "There's still time to get a hot meal up at the mess hall," he said. "But you better double-time it."

Jackson shook his head. "I got C's. Sleep is all I be needin'. I'm *beaucoup* tired. Where am I sackin' out?"

"There might be an extra cot in the supply tent. These guys have the last two in here."

"He can have mine," Brian offered.

"Or mine," Raul said.

"I won't be needin' no fuckin' cot," Jackson snarled. "I been sleepin' in foxholes and damn near every other shithole in 'Nam for the last year. I wouldn't know what to do with a cot!'

"Suit yourself," Prescott replied. "You can sleep in the supply tent next door. There are plenty of duffle bags in there to sleep on."

Jackson nodded. "What about tomorrow?"

"Got a Jeep gassed and ready for you first thing in the morning. It's all set. Once you get to the base, ask anyone for directions to the Evac Hospital."

"I know where it's at!" Jackson snarled, pointing to the scars on his face.

Prescott nodded. Jackson picked up his rucksack and went out the door, heading for the adjacent supply tent.

Scott and Arano turned to Prescott. "*Madre mía!* What the hell was that?" Arano asked the sergeant.

Prescott shook his head. "That dude is one serious piece of work. Don't even think about messin' with him."

Scott smiled. "You don't have to worry about that, Sarge."

"*Ni hablar!*" Arano agreed. "No way!"

71

"Who is he?" Scott asked.

The sergeant quickly explained. "Name's Danny Ray Jackson, a rifleman, who comes from some little, ass-backward place in West Virginia, so far out in the boonies they have to pipe the sunlight in. They say he's related to General 'Stonewall' Jackson himself. I wouldn't doubt it. Both have reputations for being hardcore, smoke-bringers!"

"No kiddin'," Brian said. "Stonewall Jackson, the Civil War general."

"Don't screw with him," Prescott warned. "The guy's a killing machine and has more enemy kills than anyone else in the entire company. He's a loner, but a living legend among the grunts. And right now, he's got a serious case of the ass, 'cause he only has about a week left in-country and the Old Man won't let him out of the bush. He's madder than all hell. And I really don't blame him."

"So, he's a short-timer," Arano said.

"Affirmative," Prescott nodded. "They don't get much shorter."

Prescott shrugged. "At first the grunts called him Danny Ray," the sergeant said, "but then, because of the KIAs he was rackin' up, they nicknamed him Danny Ray the Death Ray. Now they call him the Short-timer."

In awe, Brian muttered, "Danny Ray Jackson, the Death Ray … the Short-timer."

CHAPTER 11

"Excuse me, Captain," Lieutenant Manly said, interrupting a conference Rutkowski was having with a handful of uniformed patrolmen.

Rutkowski turned. "What is it?"

Manly had Kathy by the arm. Just behind them stood Arthur and Julie Benedict. "This is Kathy Hamilton, Brian Scott's girlfriend."

Rutkowski shook her hand. "Captain Frank Rutkowski, Ms. Hamilton. Glad to meet you." He nodded politely, then quickly dismissed the patrolmen.

After Manly introduced the Benedicts, Kathy asked, "How's Brian?"

"As far as we know, he's fine," Rutkowski said. "But I'm afraid we have a delicate situation here." He went on to fully explain the stand-off, finishing with, "So, because of the danger to him and the others, we can't just go in there. Once he lets the others go, we'll have more latitude."

"Let me go in, please," Kathy pleaded. "I know he'll talk to me. I know I can get him to let the others go. Please, let me go." Julie put her hands on Kathy's shoulders, trying to comfort her.

"I'm afraid we can't do that, Ms. Hamilton. It's too dangerous. We may ask you to talk with Brian by telephone, if we can get him to the phone."

Suddenly overwhelmed with emotion, Kathy covered her face with her hands and wept. She turned into Julie to hide her tears, and her friend hugged her close, reassuringly.

"Try not to worry so. He's going to be fine, Kathy," Julie insisted. "He's going to be fine."

"Julie is right," Arthur concurred. "This is all going to work out, and for the good, too. I know it is."

Captain Rutkowski put a hand to his aching head. "It's not unusual for situations like this to end quietly, Ms. Hamilton. It's our job to stay calm and do everything we can to keep Brian calm, too."

"I don't want anything to happen to him," Kathy said, turning to the captain. "He's a good man and I love him. He doesn't deserve to be hurt."

"I agree one hundred percent," said Rutkowski. "And I promise you we're going to do our best to make sure he doesn't get hurt. But we also have a responsibility to the hostages and their families."

"I understand," Kathy sobbed. "I just don't want him hurt."

Rutkowski stepped closer and took her hand. Holding it gently, he said, "We don't want to see anyone get hurt, Ms. Hamilton. I'm aware of Brian's Vietnam War record. Believe me, I have a soft spot in my heart for all those guys who fought in that war. My older brother was killed in a Viet Cong ambush. He's buried in a cemetery not far from here. I think about him every day."

When he finished, he gave her hand a firm squeeze, then took a step back.

"Thank you, Captain," she said, sincerely. "Thank you."

Arthur spoke up. "Any idea what's going on in there? What he's doing?"

"Yes, Doctor," said the captain. "Apparently, he's relating a story."

"A story?" Julie said, looking confused.

"That's what McGuiggan, the owner and bartender, told us when we spoke to him on the phone. He's telling a story about Vietnam. Maybe it's something he just wants to get off his chest. I don't know, but McGuiggan informed us that Brian would only talk to us after he finished his story. So, we're waiting."

Kathy recalled Brian's violent reaction when she had mentioned the Death Ray and the Short-timer. She felt certain his story might have something to do with that. But far more worrisome, she feared what might happen after he finished telling it.

"A story about Vietnam," Arthur mused aloud. "Hmmm." He turned to Kathy. "It sounds like you were right about PTSD."

Kathy nodded. "I'm certain of it."

"You think he's suffering from PTSD?" Rutkowski questioned.

"It's possible, Captain. Post-Traumatic Stress Disorder is a mental and behavior disorder that can strike combat veterans, as well as others who have experienced violent trauma. Not all war veterans get it, but many do. It appears that Brian may have been quietly suffering with it for many years. Now suddenly, after a long delay, it has manifested in an acute form."

Rutkowski listened intently. "Delayed," he said, "Then brought on—how, why?"

"The why is the difficult part, but how it's brought on—well, it could have been something that reminded Brian of a traumatic incident in Vietnam. A helicopter passing over head, a rainy day, a dark tree line, it's hard to pinpoint what could have triggered it. Perhaps, as Kathy believes, it was the stress and worry brought on by the runup to the Gulf War. Until we get Brian under our care, we can only speculate."

A sudden commotion up the block on Market Street drew everyone's attention. Lieutenant Manly quickly interrupted, "Vinton's here, Captain!"

Rutkowski watched as two, somber looking black vans carrying the SWAT team parked along Market Street. Lieutenant Russell Vinton was the first to emerge.

"My headache just took a turn for the worse. Any luck with those aspirin, Lieutenant?"

"No, but I haven't given up."

Rutkowski rubbed his temples, as the Lieutenant went on. "We've got someone who knows the entire layout inside McGuiggan's."

"Who is it?"

75

"The cook. She was coming to work; says she knows the place like the back of her hand."

"Good, keep her close in case we need her."

The Lieutenant nodded, as the SWAT team members began spilling out onto the street. Watching them in their black camo uniforms, Kathy started to sob again. Arthur and Julie held her hands, trying to allay her fears.

"Doctor Benedict," Rutkowski announced, "I'd like you to hang loose here. I want to talk with you a little more about PTSD. And Ms. Hamilton, I'd like you to stand by also. We may need your help with Brian. We might ask you to speak with him. Now, I have to take care of some other business. You're welcome to wait in my car, out of this drizzle." He turned to Manly. "John, do we have any coffee here?"

"No, Captain," Manly shook his head, "but I can see about getting some."

"Yes, please, put someone on it. How about Victor 60?"

Victor 60, or Vehicle 60, was the Department's mobile office, and nothing more than a barebones, outdated thirty-foot trailer pulled by a pickup truck.

"It's on the way," Manly snapped. "Should be here any minute."

"Good, now let's go talk with General Patton, I mean Lieutenant Vinton."

Kathy refused to get into the police car and insisted on staying out on the street. Captain Rutkowski and Lieutenant Manly excused themselves and walked the short distance up Market Street to talk with the SWAT commander.

CHAPTER 12

Inside McGuiggan's, in the same intense, trance-like manner, Brian Scott continued with his story:

"I don't get it," Brian complained to Sergeant Prescott, "if the guy's so short, and they normally send guys like that back here to the rear and out of harm's way, why not Jackson?"

"Yeah, Sarge," Arano chimed in. "Is there something more going on?"

Prescott had grabbed a rag and dropped it over Jackson's tobacco saliva on the wood floor. "Well, only the Old Man knows for sure," he said, pushing the rag around with his boot. "But it wouldn't surprise me if he was doing it out of spite."

"How so?" Brian asked. "Why would he do that?"

"Don't repeat me on this," the sergeant said in a lowered voice. "But the Old Man and most of the other officers and NCOs in the outfit have had a case of the ass against Jackson at one time or another. Hell, you saw the way he was in here!" The sergeant picked up the rag and tossed it into a waste can by his desk. "Nasty tobacco juice!" he grimaced. "Jackson is a rough cut, smart as a fox, and as crafty as one, too. But he's been known to buck authority, even criticize policy and tactics—more so than the normal bitching coming from regular troops. And it's earned him a lot of critics. He tells it like it is and doesn't care who he tells. That's why he's still a PFC. But ..." The sergeant paused for a moment to chuckle, before finishing, "But, if the truth be known, there ain't one of them who don't admire him for his hardcore courage and can-do ability. Not a one of them."

"*Hijole!*" Arano said. "That's the price you pay for speaking your mind. Unfortunately, the Army's no different than anywhere else."

"Pretty damn sorry," Brian added. "Pretty damn sorry."

Later that night, before Brian and Raul turned in, Sergeant Prescott gave them a short tutorial about radio watch for the night—what to do and what to listen for.

"Wake me up if the company reports any sort of problem during the night," he told them. "I'll take the first watch. Arano, you take the second, and after your hour is done, wake up Scott for his turn. We'll continue that way through the night. Sit here by the radio and don't fall asleep. Got it?"

"Got it, Sarge," the two new men said.

Afterward, fully clothed with their boots on and their newly issued M-16s by their sides, Scott and Arano slipped through the mosquito net covering and got into their cots, ready for sleep. But as the night progressed, the two got very little sleep. Random firing came from the bunker line along the perimeter of the base, and flares went up and popped off every so often. There was near constant radio chatter within the hooch. Mosquitoes infiltrated the netting and attacked them, and Sergeant Prescott talked in his sleep about a "sweet, true-fine" woman he had mistakenly left for another. The two men felt the stress and anxiety of their first night away from the safety of the reception center in Chu Lai. Both lay restless in their cots, wet with sweat and thinking of a thousand things, especially their odds for survival and getting home in twelve months, which now seemed more like twelve years. In short, it was a long, stress-filled, sleepless night for them. Just next door, in the supply tent, the Short-timer, Jackson, slept as peacefully as a newborn baby, sawing Zzzzs, as the grunts called it, all the night through.

At daybreak, Sergeant Prescott rousted Scott and Arano out of their cots and they went outside to the side of the hooch to hit the "piss tube" that was half sunk into the ground. After chow at the mess hall, they returned to the hooch. At 0800 hours, Prescott led them outside, where Jackson, with his M-16 leaning next to him, sat on a couple sandbags by the supply tent, eating C-rations with a plastic spoon. When he finished, he took a swig of water from a dirty canteen. Deep in his own thoughts, he didn't speak to the others when they came out.

"I'll be back in a minute," Prescott told Scott and Arano. "You guys just hang tight with Jackson here." He walked off in the direction of the mess hall.

Scott and Arano stood by uncomfortably, glancing at each other and Jackson, who continued to eat in silence. *He's probably thinking of home*, Scott thought, before speaking up. "Good morning, Jackson," he said, smiling at him. "How'd you sleep last night?"

Jackson had just put a plug of tobacco in his mouth. Nodding, he said, "Like a fuckin' babysan!"

Minutes later, Prescott pulled up in a Jeep and parked in front of the hooch. Leaving the motor running, he jumped out.

"There you go, Jackson," the sergeant said. "You sure you remember how to get there?"

The Death Ray gave him a hard look, and said, "Mrs. Jackson didn't raise no idiots. It's just a hoot an' a holler up Highway One. A blind man could find it!"

Scott and Arano turned away, trying not to laugh. They weren't used to hearing anyone talk to a sergeant like that.

"Ok," Prescott said. "Hop in and get going." He turned to the two new men. "You guys get in the back. They're going with you, Jackson. Drop them at Brigade finance. They have some forms to re-do. Bring them back when you come."

Jackson flared up immediately. "I ain't takin' these new guys," he said, glaring at Prescott. "They're nothin' but bad luck."

Prescott stiffened. "You don't have a choice," he snapped. "You gotta take them. How else are they gonna get there?'

"They can hump it for all I care!" Jackson spit tobacco juice onto the dirt road.

"They're going with you and that's an order!" Prescott turned to Scott and Arano. "Go ahead. You men get in the Jeep."

The two quickly followed the sergeant's command. They sat quietly in the back of the open-air vehicle, waiting to see what Jackson was going to do. In a moment, they had their answer.

"More Army bullshit," the West Virginian snarled, throwing his M-16 into the Jeep, and climbing in behind the wheel. He gunned the motor, shifted into first, and popped the clutch. The Jeep jerked forward with tires roaring, sending a cloud of dusty dirt into the air behind them.

Prescott covered his nose and mouth and watched the Jeep speed off. "That guy is one pissed off trooper!" he muttered.

In little time, the unlikely trio cleared the LZ's gate and made their way onto Highway One, where Scott and Arano noticed the same circus of travelers they had seen the day before. Inside the windswept Jeep, the atmosphere was tense and quiet. Still angry, Jackson drove in silence. Scott and Arano didn't speak to him. As new grunts, with no combat experience, they felt intimidated by any seasoned grunt, but the Death Ray had such a frightening aura about him, that they felt it more acutely. In short, he spooked them, and in no way did they want to make him angrier than he was already.

Up ahead, a dilapidated old truck chugged along the highway, going north like them. It raised a trail of dusty dirt and spewed a smelly, gray cloud of burnt engine oil. Vietnamese civilians in black pajamas covered it like ants. They filled the open truck bed, clung to the sides, and packed the running boards and bumpers. Scott and Arano watched the truck and the people on it with great curiosity, but got the impression that it was not an unusual sight at all on Highway One.

A small boy, a babysan, suddenly fell off the side of the truck and bounced to a sitting position onto his behind, where he sat in the brown dirt crying and watching the truck continue without him. An old mamasan in black pajamas and conical hat, still on board, waved and screamed frantically at the boy, who got up and ran after the truck. Riders screamed at the driver to stop, while others screamed at the boy. Ignoring the ruckus, the driver kept the overloaded truck lumbering on as if nothing had happened. Finally, the mamasan jumped off the truck and ran toward the boy.

The three soldiers watched the little drama unfold before them.

"Goddamned Vietnamese," Jackson complained, hitting the gas and speeding toward the two castoffs. With his bandana flapping in the wind, he quickly came alongside them, then hit the brakes hard to bring the Jeep to a sudden stop.

"Get in, get in!" he shouted to the mamasan, pointing to the empty passenger's seat. Frightened, the old woman clutched the boy's hand and backed away from the Jeep.

"*Lai dai, lai dai!*" Jackson shouted at them. "Git over here, *lai dai*, git here!" He shouted again and again, while pointing to the empty seat and revving the motor. But woman was too scared to move. Frustrated, Jackson put the Jeep in neutral, grabbed his M-16, and jumped out. Scott and Arano watched intently, wondering what he was going to do.

Seeing the weapon, the mamasan became frantic. She held the boy close and screamed. Ignoring her cries, Jackson used the barrel of his rifle to prod her to the Jeep and to point to the fleeing truck. Finally, she grasped his intention and stopped crying. She picked up the boy and carried him to the Jeep.

"Y'all help 'em in," Jackson hollered to Scott and Arano. The two jumped out immediately. Arano held the boy, while Scott helped the woman into the seat, then Arano handed her the little boy. After the two climbed back in, Jackson hit the gas and the Jeep sped off.

Easily catching the slow-moving truck, he pulled alongside and motioned to the driver to stop, but the old, goateed papasan ignored him.

"What the hell!" Jackson hollered. "*Dung lai, dung lai*! Stop that truck, ya ol' sonuvabitch!"

Scott, Arano and the mamasan hollered at the driver, too, and motioned for him to stop. But the stubborn man ignored them, angering Jackson. He stomped his foot on the gas pedal and the Jeep lurched forward again. The occupants held on for dear life as he sped past the truck, then cut in front of it and hit the brakes, forcing the truck driver to come to a hard stop that jostled his passengers.

With his M-16, Danny Ray leaped out of the Jeep, cursing and threatening the truck driver, who lowered his head and cowered behind the wheel, shaking nervously. Jackson shouted to Scott and Arano, "Ya'll un-ass that Jeep, and get 'em on the truck! C'mon, move it!"

The Vietnamese onlookers laughed and cheered as the two men helped the mamasan and child back to the truck. Two elderly papasans lent a hand and pulled them back on board. When they were safely on, the crowd cheered all the louder. Now showing big smiles, the woman and the boy waved to Danny Ray as he hit the gas pedal and left the truck behind in a cloud of Highway One dust.

"Damned, crazy Vietnamese," Jackson complained.

Minutes later, up ahead on the right, the entrance to the Chu Lai military base came into view, but Jackson gave his two companions another surprise when, instead of turning in to the heavily secured gate, he drove straight past it.

Arano poked Scott and gave him a questioning look. Neither had any idea why he didn't turn into the base.

Maybe he knows of another entrance, they wondered. *Or maybe he's up to something else.*

When he passed the northern most point of the base, where its outer defensive ring of barbed wire and sandbagged bunkers arced east toward the coast, Jackson still hadn't given them an explanation. Soon he drove into a village of ramshackle, broken-down hooches and shops that straddled both sides of the widened roadway. Cruising on through the village, they saw many Vietnamese civilians in black pajamas, strolling along the sides of the road, going in and out of the shops and hooches. There was a sprinkling of ARVN and Popular Force soldiers among them, all wearing OD green fatigues. Going on, they passed open-air markets and a roadside barbershop, where a short line of ARVNs waited for an ancient barber to cut their hair.

Nearly all of the ARVNs and the PFs carried rifles, which made Scott and Arano a little nervous. But when Jackson paid them little mind, they felt a little less worried.

Toward the end of the shopping thoroughfare, Jackson turned left into an alley running between two corrugated tin-roofed hooches, sending a gathering of chickens scurrying noisily out of his way. On emerging from the alley, he turned right and continued past the rear of three shops before parking behind one of the largest hooches in the ville. Danny Ray quickly got out, taking the keys and his M-16 with him.

"Gotta quick stop to make," he muttered. "Y'all can come with me or stay here. Yer call. If'n ya come in, don't eat or drink anythin'!"

He threw his rifle onto his shoulder, and holding the barrel with his right hand, walked toward the hooch, then quickly entered a narrow walkway between the hooches and followed it back out front to the dusty, shopping promenade.

"*Ay, caramba!*" Arano said, grabbing his M-16. "I don't know about you, Brian, but I'm not stayin' here." He hurried after Jackson.

"Me neither!" Scott said, going after him with his rifle.

They were only steps behind him when he went into the hooch. A painting of a blue butterfly and the words *Con bướm xanh* stood out on a sign by the door. They had no idea what kind of a place it was, but going inside, they were surprised to see Jackson standing by a small bar, talking to a middle-aged Vietnamese woman with black hair and black teeth. On the wall behind the bar, an array of liquor bottles sat on wooden shelves, and a few round tables and some chairs were arranged in the room for patrons.

"G.I. want beer?" the old woman said to Jackson. "We have Tiger beer. Number huckin' one. Berry, berry good and beaucoup cold."

Danny Ray put a hand up to her. "Vietnam beer number ten," he snapped. "Vietnam boom-boom, number one!"

The woman smiled. "Ah," she said, nodding her head knowingly. "GI want boom-boom. Number huckin' one in Blue Butterfly! You come with me. Me got girl for you."

She started to escort him to an aisle leading to a hallway that led past the bar and into a separated back section of the rickety old hooch, when he stopped and turned back to Scott and Arano.

"Y'all can wait in here or outside," he called. "See any MP's a-comin', give me a holler, ASAP. This place is off-limits. MP's show, we beat feet."

As Danny Ray disappeared into the back with the old woman, a surly looking, black-pajama-clad bartender came in from the back. Just moments later, two other G.I. patrons came in the front door. "Tiger beers," they called to the bartender.

The men, one with an M-16 and the other with a .45 on his pistol belt, took seats at one of the tables in the room and lit cigarettes. Scott and Arano nodded to them before going outside to wait on Jackson.

"Boom-boom," Arano chuckled as the two stood in the hot sun at the front of the bar. "*Madre mía!* Jackson is somethin' else."

"Agreed!" Scott replied with a laugh. "And did you check out that bartender?"

"*Hijole!*" Arano shook his head. "Nasty lookin' dude."

The two went on passing the minutes in small talk about Vietnam, Jackson and Sergeant Prescott. Then Arano said something that really shook his friend.

"'I got a bad feelin' about this place, Brian," he confided in a serious tone.

"You mean this crappy bar or Vietnam?"

"Vietnam!"

"In what way?"

Arano glanced down the street before he replied. "I got this creepy feelin' that I'm never going to make it out of here alive!"

Scott looked surprised. "What? No way, *Amigo*," he said. "I've had the same feeling, and I'd bet every grunt who ever set foot in this country has had the same creepy feeling. So, don't sweat it. You're not alone. Not by a long shot."

"Yeah, I thought about that, too," Arano said. "Still, I just can't shake the feeling that I'm going to die here."

"Bullshit!" Scott snapped, angrily. "That's bullshit, man."

Suddenly, a commotion inside the bar interrupted their conversation.

"Sounds like a fight!" Scott said, going for the door. Alarmed, they quickly went back inside to see what was going on.

The soldier with the .45 was standing by his table, clutching his throat. He had knocked over his chair, and his beer bottle lay on its side on the tabletop.

"What's wrong?" his buddy asked him, trying to help.

"My throat!" the man gasped, leaning forward on the table, but the panicky victim wouldn't let him near.

Then, wild-eyed and looking like the Death Ray, Jackson rushed back into the barroom with his M-16. His sweat-soaked shirt hung open, and a half-dressed and frightened Vietnamese girl followed behind him. Scott and Arano backed out of the way, wondering what was going on and why the man was in such distress.

Then the mamason came in, shouting incoherently in Vietnamese at the man behind the bar, who glared at her angrily. The gasping man dropped into a chair and hung his head painfully between his knees as if he were going to throw up. Saliva oozed from his mouth. His friend knelt next to him, trying to get him to say what was wrong.

Danny Ray went to the table where the two had been sitting and picked up the man's beer bottle. He held it to his nose, smelling it suspiciously. He poured a small puddle of beer onto the tabletop, and sifted through it with his fingers, then put them to his nose. Still arguing loudly, the bartender and woman kept a wary eye on Jackson, while Scott and Arano watched him, too. They wondered what he was searching for. They noticed a jittery panic about the old woman as she jabbered more excitedly to the bartender. Then, the girl suddenly shouted something, turned, and ran for the back of the hooch.

Something's not right! the new men instinctively thought.

Jackson's expression changed from one of suspicion to hot anger. The bartender and mamasan noted it immediately. Turning toward them, he shouted accusingly, "VC!"

The bartender brought up a pistol from below the bar, confirming Jackson's suspicions. He quickly crouched and raised his M-16, and they fired simultaneously at one another. Clutching his chest, the bartender slammed backward into the assortment of liquor bottles, crying out in pain. He fell to the floor with a thud, taking a half dozen of the bottles with him. The two rounds he got off at Jackson had gone harmlessly through the wall. In semi-shock, Scott and Arano had backed out of the way, never thinking of using their weapons.

The mamasan ran for the back of the hooch, and the West Virginian turned and fired another short burst from his rifle. The woman screamed, but no one could see if she had been hit.

Jackson checked the soldier, who was still seated in a painful stupor, then turned to his friend. "We'll git help!" he said. "Yer buddy's been snake bit! They spiked his beer." He held up his hand, rubbing his fingers together. "Glass, metal shavings, maybe poison, too." He turned and walked out the front door, with Scott and Arano trailing behind. A crowd of Vietnamese civilians had quickly formed in front of the bar, curious about the shooting. Jackson, with his two apprentices, walked calmly into the crowd, causing the people to part as if the Israelites were passing through the Red Sea. Returning to their Jeep, Jackson tossed his M-16 inside and jumped in. Scott and Arano got in, and he drove off, taking his time through the alley, and back onto Highway One, where it ran through the shopping promenade. He drove at a slow, inconspicuous rate of speed.

On their way out of the village, they spotted an MP Jeep coming toward them. "Y'all don't say shit!" Jackson warned his passengers. Then as the Jeeps closed in on one another, the two MP occupants waved them down.

Motors running, the Jeeps stopped alongside each other. "Everything copacetic?" the burly sergeant behind the wheel asked Jackson, looking the three over suspiciously.

"Fine as grandpa's shine in the summertime, Sarge," Jackson said with a pleasant grin.

"What's your business here in the ville?"

"None," he said matter-of-factly. "We're on our way to Chu Lai and jest thought we'd do a little sightseein'. That's all."

"Well, you guys better get a move on. VC may be in the ville!"

"No shit!" Jackson said, feigning surprise. "Thank ya for the warnin'. We're outta here." Jackson put the Jeep in gear, but suddenly turned back to the MPs. "Yo," he said, "back up the road apiece, we drove by a hooch with a blue butterfly on it. Saw a couple of our guys go in. Now there's a crowd out front. Y'all might wanna check it out."

The two military policemen, glanced at one another knowingly. Then the sergeant said, "VC joint. They messed up a grunt in there a couple days ago. Thanks. We'll check it out."

The MPs took off for the bar, while Jackson popped the clutch and sped out of the village, heading for Brigade finance and the Evac Hospital in Chu Lai. He never said a word to Scott and Arano about what had happened in the bar, and they didn't say anything to him about it.

. . .

In McGuiggan's, Brian stopped his narration and sat motionless, staring at the front door. The others sat quietly too, digesting the incredible incident he had just recounted. After a few moments, Cheryl broke the silence. "Is that the story you wanted to tell?" she asked.

Seemingly more aware of his surroundings and out of his stupor, Brian turned to her with moistened eyes. "It's part of it," he said. And after a brief, thoughtful pause, he added, "I wish to God that was all of it!"

87

CHAPTER 13

"Listen up, men," 36-year-old Lieutenant Russel Vinton said to the members of his Wilmington SWAT team. "Draw your weapons and ammo from the supply van and get ready to deploy! Team Leader, make sure everyone checks out." Without hesitation, Vinton's men followed his orders, while the cigar-smoking Lieutenant checked over his Colt SMG, 9mm rifle. Seeing Rutkowski and Manly approaching, he slung the weapon and saluted the captain.

"Well, Frank," Vinton said, blowing cigar smoke, "what kind of a cluster-fuck operation do we have here?"

Vinton's close cropped blond hair made a stark contrast with his black camo uniform. Ignoring his comment, Rutkowski and Manly briefed him on the situation, then they called on McGuiggan's cook to give them the layout of the bar. The matronly woman provided a detailed description of the inside of the building, including the basement and second floor.

"It's not a big place," she concluded, "and like I said, there's only two ways in—the front door and the back door, which Paddy is a pain in the ass about always keepin' locked."

When she was finished and had answered all their questions, they thanked her and asked her to stay for a while longer. She readily agreed, after which they quickly excused her and continued with their pow-wow.

"Three people in there with him, right?" Vinton said to Rutkowski.

"Yeah, Russ, according to our street guys who were inside."

"And he's a 'Nam vet?"

Manly nodded, "Bronze Star for bravery."

Vinton glanced down Market Street towards McGuiggan's. He tossed his cigar and spit. "You've got uniforms down there?"

"Couple men out front, couple in back. When you're ready to deploy, we'll pull them out. We've disabled his truck in case he decides to take a hike."

Vinton shook his head. "Seen it happen one time," he said, mysteriously.

"What's that?"

"Situation similar to this—cops back so far somebody took their eyes off the front door and the shooter waltzed out, got into his vehicle and drove off." The SWAT leader cracked a smile. "Bunch of dip-shits!"

"That's why we're doing it this way, Russ," Rutkowski said. "And by the way, our man Scott is not a shooter. Keep that in mind. He hasn't fired a single shot."

Vinton's smile vanished. "He's got a gun and hostages—he's a shooter."

"He's a troubled veteran!" Manly affirmed, taking a half-step closer to Vinton.

"Nobody asked you, Manly!"

Rutkowski stepped between the two and took Vinton by the arm. "Your team's safety and that of the hostages come first, Russ. Make no mistake about it! But this guy is a decorated war veteran with a problem, and I personally promised his girlfriend that I'd do all I could to keep him safe. You can walk right down there and take one look into that girl's eyes and see how worried she is and how much she loves the guy. I mean to keep that promise! Understand?" The captain was squeezing his arm by the time he finished.

"Roger, Captain," Vinton replied, pulling his arm free. "I got it."

Vinton's team leader, a sergeant, stepped over and interrupted. "Lieutenant, the men are ready. Weapons, equipment, communications, everything checks."

Vinton nodded. "Okay, I'll be right there."

The sergeant left and rejoined the rest of the team.

"Okay, Frank, I've got eight guys, including my snipers. I'll be in front with two. We'll have the ram. I'll put three men at the rear and the snipers on the high ground, front and back. Nobody in my team makes a move unless I say so, and I'll coordinate everything with you."

Rutkowski and Manly nodded. "Right," said the captain. "And remember, I'm calling the shots here, Russ. We've got to make sure we're all on the same page. No room for mavericks. That's how people get hurt."

Russ Vinton nodded. "I'm with ya, Frank!"

"Good. Now it's just a waiting game. Hostage Negotiations should be here any minute now. Once they arrive, we'll try another phone call; try talking to him again."

The SWAT commander nodded. "No problem. Best thing that could happen, he puts his weapon down and comes out with his hands up, just like in the movies. But if he decides to pull the trigger—and there's a pretty good chance he will—then it's a whole different matter, Frank. We better be ready to get in there in a hurry, and you better be ready to give the command, or it'll be your ass that they nail to the wall. Not mine!"

The confab was suddenly interrupted by a media cameraman who came from upper Market Street and had somehow gotten past the barricade.

"Somebody get that guy out of here!" Rutkowski bawled, pointing to the man and showing his irritation.

Lieutenant Manly called two nearby uniformed officers and signaled them to escort the intruder back beyond the barrier.

"Media!" the captain complained, turning his back on the cameraman and rubbing his temples. "Damned media ... damned headache! I get your message, Russ, now get your men moving."

Vinton saluted and rejoined his team of specialists.

Rutkowski and Manly watched for a few moments as the SWAT crew geared-up, pulling on black, fire-protective hoods and military style helmets. As Vinton briefed them, the members checked their weapons one last time. The two, crack-shot snipers carried .308, bolt-action rifles that were equipped with night assistance scopes. One member of the team carried a 12-gauge shotgun and the others carried 9 mm rifles with extra magazines. Each man was also armed with a 9 mm pistol. In addition, the team had a tear gas gun and flash bangs, that could be used as distractors.

After the final weapons inspection, Vinton did one last communications check to make certain the radios were working properly.

"Patton and his Third Army," Lieutenant Manly said.

"Yeah, but we couldn't operate without them!" Rutkowski noted. The captain took his young lieutenant friend by the arm and confided in him. "I know how you feel about Vinton, John, but in a shoot-'em-up, I'd want him in my corner. I couldn't say that about a lot of guys. In his own way, he's a damn good man. He's just a little, how did you put it?"

"Intense, Captain."

"Yeah," Rutkowski smiled, shaking his head, "just a little too intense."

. . .

On Captain Rutkowski's order, the uniformed officers pulled back toward the Command Post on Market Street. After one of his snipers took up a position to cover McGuiggan's front door, Vinton and his men moved out, a file of silent shadows, crossing Second Street. Kathy Hamilton, trembling with worry, watched the heavily armed men make their way toward McGuiggan's.

"If anything happens to Brian," she said to Arthur and Julie. "I don't know what I'll do."

Julie hugged her and gently rocked back and forth. "It's going to be all right," she said with confidence. "Any minute now Brian's going to come out, and this will all be over."

91

The husband-and-wife team tried to coax Kathy out of the light rain, but she refused. "I want to be here in case Brian needs me," she said.

Vinton and two of his men peeled away from the file and turned east up Second Street, hugging the building fronts, and making their way toward the entrance to the pub. The remaining members, under the close direction of the team leader, kept going. They made their way behind the row of buildings, where they took concealed positions to cover the bar's rear exit. The team leader then sent his remaining sniper into position. Once the men were all in place, Vinton ran another radio check with his team and with Rutkowski's Command Post on Market Street. Everything checked out okay. All was ready.

. . .

Back in McGuiggan's, Brian kept closed court with his spellbound listeners, relating his story. "If that was the whole story," he said, sorrowfully, "I wouldn't be sitting here now, a miserable, worthless son of a bitch!"

After another silent pause, Paddy spoke up, asking, "Did anything happen to Danny Ray for shooting the guy and the old woman?"

"No," Brian shook his head. "Raul and I never said anything about it. We figured they were VC, Viet Cong, and that's just the way things went in 'Nam. People got killed no matter which side they were on."

"If that's not it, then what is it you want to get off your chest?" Mark asked, picking up his nearly empty glass. Paddy got up and quickly filled Mark's glass and topped off the others. Brian continued with his story.

"We finished our business in Chu Lai, and Danny Ray got us back to Badger around noon. After chow, Sergeant Prescott told us that a chopper was going to pick up all three of us and fly us out to Bravo Company, fourteen or so miles northwest of Badger. He said the grunts nicknamed the place Knee Deep Valley because it's crawling with Viet Cong and NVA, and it was the place where the company got the two enemy machine guns sitting out front of the hooch. In short, Prescott said it was a dangerous place, and the reason Jackson, the Short-timer, had such a case of the ass.

"The afternoon turned into the old Army game of hurry-up-and-wait. We hung around most of the day waiting for the chopper. I don't know what Jackson and Arano were thinking about as we sat killing time, but I was filled with worry and apprehension. Prescott's words about the Valley crawling with the enemy really spooked me and kept echoing in my head. I was going to get my baptism of fire in a miserable, dangerous place they called Knee Deep Valley. I wasn't eager for it, but I was ready."

Then filling with emotion, Scott lowered his head and wept once again. The others surmised that he was getting closer to some horrible revelation in his narrative. Something exceptionally dark that had hounded him for years seemed to be pushing him to the brink. They exchanged glances of compassion for the troubled veteran, yet they were too frightened to utter a sympathetic word of comfort to him or do anything to allay his misery. Instead, they sat locked in fear, with one eye on the broken, dispirited warrior and one eye on his terrifying handgun.

Then, Scott looked up and cried, "I wish to God that I had never gone to that damn valley!"

CHAPTER 14

A uniformed officer called out to Rutkowski. "Negotiations people are here, Captain!"

Rutkowski and Manly turned to see Lieutenant Nora Henderson driving down Market Street toward the CP. Accompanying her were Patrolman Stan Martin and Sergeant Ronnie Okine. Martin was the team's Talker, who negotiated directly with the hostage-taker, while Okine was the Coach. He would listen in on Martin's conversation and support him by doing the behind the scenes negotiating with the department, city officials, and any other organization, group or person mentioned in the perpetrator's demands. Lieutenant Henderson was the leader and overall coordinator.

Rutkowski greeted the team, and once again detailed the situation to the lieutenant.

"We've called for Victor 60 and when it shows, we'll have a place to set up out of this lousy rain."

Henderson nodded. "Any family members or friends here?" she asked, with briefcase in hand. "Anyone who can help talk him out of there?"

"No family members," said Rutkowski, "but his girlfriend is here, and two friends, a psychologist from the Veterans Hospital and his wife, who is an RN there." The captain pointed to Kathy and the Benedicts huddled in front of a darkened storefront drinking coffee.

"They could be a real help," Henderson said, noting the group. "If there's nothing further, I think we'll go meet with them while we're waiting for Victor 60."

"No, nothing more," Rutkowski said, "except good luck!"

Henderson smiled. Manly spoke up. "Come on, I'll introduce you."

They started off, but Rutkowski suddenly stopped them.

"Before you go, Lieutenant, you wouldn't happen to have any aspirin in your briefcase? I've got one hell of a headache."

"Sorry, Captain," she replied.

Rutkowski grimaced and put a hand to his aching head.

At Fourth and Market, just a short way up the street, Victor 60 suddenly appeared. Officers manning the barricade at the intersection let it pass onto Market Street.

"There's a good sign." Rutkowski said.

In a matter of minutes, the trailer would become the new Command Post, complete with heat, electricity, and communications equipment.

Rutkowski had all his players nearly in position now. One he was unaware of, Brian Scott's father, had just arrived at the barricade on Fourth Street.

No sooner had Mr. Scott shown up, than the screeching of tires and a sudden loud crash echoed down Market Street, coming from further up the street.

"Sounds like we might have another complication!" the captain said to one of the nearby uniformed officers.

"Hope none of our guys were involved."

"See what you can find out about it!" Rutkowski said to the man, rubbing his aching head. "No wonder I have a headache."

Minutes later, the alarm at a nearby fire station went off. *EMTs on the way*, he surmised.

. . .

In McGuiggan's, Brian once again tipped over into a psychotic-like state where his relationship to the here and now seemed to vanish. As he resumed his spellbinding account, he didn't just retell the memory as a foggy, fragmented recollection, but rather, he told it with such anguished detail and emotional intensity, that it seemed as if he were re-living the event in real time. His impassioned concentration and intensity had a uniquely profound effect on his listeners, too, as they were swept into the incredible narrative.

. . .

Late that afternoon, Sergeant Prescott received the radio call that they had been waiting for. The chopper was on the way!

"Saddle up, men," Prescott said. "Bird's on the way."

Scott, Arano and Jackson put on their rucksacks and steel pot helmets, then picked up their M-16s.

"I wish you two guys the very best," Prescott said to the new men. "Stay low and keep your heads down. Watch Jackson and learn from him. If the shit hits the fan, you won't find a better tutor out there."

The two men thanked Prescott, who then turned to Danny Ray. "Take care of these two, Jackson," the supply sergeant said, "and watch out for yourself. Most likely you'll be back in a few days to clear base and go home. So, watch out!"

Jackson nodded, then went out the door.

Scott and Arano thanked the sergeant again, before going after Jackson and following him to the landing zone.

Minutes later the whoop, whoop, whoop sound of the approaching chopper echoed over the LZ. By the time it landed, the three were there and waiting on one knee. Jackson climbed into the open cargo bay first, then Scott and Arano. The pilots gave them a thumbs up, and the chopper took off, raising a windstorm of dust and dirt as it gained altitude.

Scott and Arano sat nervously on the floor, as they started their first chopper ride in 'Nam. They leaned back against their rucksacks, watching the countryside below them, especially the coastline with its ribbon of beautiful white sand and the blue green South China Sea. The scene looked like a resort in paradise. Soon, however, as they got farther from the coast, the scenic views changed into dull, monotonous rice paddies, then rolling hills, and finally to rugged, jungle-covered mountains. Strangely enough, the sky transformed too, going from bright and sunny to gray and overcast, bringing an ominous shadow of trepidation over the two.

What's it going to be like? they wondered. *Are we going right into combat? Will I hold up? Do I have enough ammo?* So many worries and doubts brought on so many questions.

Moments after taking off, the oppressive heat was gone, replaced by cool air that steadily blew through the open chopper, refreshing the men with nature's air conditioning. Scott and Arano watched Jackson as he sat on the floor with his legs dangling out into the wind and his bandanna flapping. He held his M-16 between his legs, pointed groundward, with a finger pressed lightly against the trigger. The two rookies found themselves wondering how many times he'd flown into combat. They found themselves wishing they had his confidence and experience—his flair and fearless attitude, too.

What's he thinking about? Scott wondered. *The coming operation? Going home? His anger at the Old Man?*

Jackson was mum throughout the flight, not saying a word to either of them, or to the pilots and door gunners. He sat statue-like, emotionless, staring at the approaching terrain.

Scott and Arano pondered the coming year and what it would bring, and the impact it would have on them. Arano's dark premonition of his death swept over him once again. The two also couldn't help wondering if they were destined to become like Danny Ray Jackson, the Death Ray.

When the chopper finally came up on a long valley, the pilot pointed down and gave a thumbs-up to his co-pilot, indicating they had arrived and were close to their drop point. On the radio, the pilot spoke with the troops on the ground, but neither Scott nor Arano could hear any of the conversation because of the roaring wind and noise from the whirling chopper blades. Going straight up the valley, the pilot shouted back to the three infantrymen, but they could barely hear anything he said. Instinctively, however, they knew he was telling them to be ready to get out of the bird. Then, with no warning, gunfire erupted on the hillside, as two hidden enemy opened fire on the chopper with AK-47 rifles. Both door gunners returned fire with their M-60 machineguns, startling the bejesus out of Scott and Arano. As tracer rounds zipped up past the chopper, they frantically looked for cover, but with none to be had, they prayed a round didn't rip through the chopper floor and kill them.

During the long-distance firefight, Jackson sat steady in his ringside seat, holding his fire, and not flinching or moving an inch, seemingly unconcerned about the rounds zipping past the bird. His hardened, flinty expression didn't change, and gave no evidence of surprise or fear.

The chopper soared downward, then leveled out and banked over the treetops. The door gunners stopped firing as abruptly as they had started. A plume of purple smoke appeared at the base of the mountains on the valley floor near the jungle's edge, marking the landing zone. The pilot circled back, then brought the chopper down on the smoke, coming in nose to nose with a lone grunt who arose from the ground to guide the bird in. The pilot had barely brought the craft to a hover, when Jackson jumped out, running in a crouch for the trees.

The pilot and the co-pilot hollered at Scott and Arano to get the hell out.

"Go, go! Get out!" the nearest door gunner screamed impatiently. "You guys tryin' to get us shot up? *Di-di! Di-di!*"

The soldier who had guided the chopper in, still in the open ground, yelled at them, "Un-ass the chopper. Come on!" He waved to the two to get out, then he turned and ran for the tree line, shouting, "*Di-di mau!* Follow me! Keep your heads down."

A hovering chopper was at its most vulnerable, like a sitting duck in a shooting gallery. Scott and Arano struggled to get up. When they jumped out, the crushing heat and humidity hit them hard, like a heart attack. The chopper lifted off immediately, its rotor blades clattering and creating a roaring whirlwind that kicked up grass, dirt, and other dead vegetation. Running for the tree line, Scott tripped and fell, but got up and kept running. Arano's helmet bounced off his head, but he quickly retrieved it, and resumed his dash for the trees.

As the chopper banked toward the hill and the trees, the two enemy gunners opened-up on it again with their AKs. A few rounds slammed into the side of the craft close to a door gunner, who was already returning fire. The firefight ended quickly as the chopper continued its climb higher up the hillside, and the enemy gunners lost sight of it due to thick foliage of the trees.

Scott and Arano ran into the tree line. Winded, they took a knee and struggled to get their breath. With the chopper gone and the shooting over, the unnerving silence of the jungle quickly set in. They had little time to recover before the squad leader called his ragged jungle rats together for the climb back up the hill.

Some of the old-timers in his squad couldn't help razzing Jackson. "Hey, Short-timer, welcome back!" one said with a laugh. "The Death Ray is so short, he's gotta reach up to tie his jungle boots!"

"Yeah," another joked, "He's so short, he's gonna need a ladder to get out of his foxhole tonight."

But Jackson didn't find much humor in the comments, and neither did Sergeant Wilson, the squad leader.

"All right, knock off the bullshit," he chided his men. He turned to Scott and Arano and introduced himself, then said, "Bravo Company is up on the hilltop, digging in for the night. There's no way a chopper could land up there so the Old Man sent us down here to bring you guys back up. He'll give you a more formal welcome when we get up there, and assign you to a platoon. So, hold any questions for him. Now, we're movin' out. It's gonna be a bitch of a climb."

"Then we best git ta humpin," Jackson interrupted, spitting brown tobacco juice onto the ground. He was standing near, leaning on his M-16 like a cane. The buck sergeant nodded to him, then sounding almost sympathetic, said, "I know you're pissed, Jackson. And I can't blame you, but what can I say? It is what it is. Just stay low and be careful. You'll be outta this shit in a couple days."

Without saying a word, Jackson lowered his head and spit again.

He had to be angry, Wilson thought. *The Old Man should have excused him from this operation back into the valley. Every time we come out here, we get into some bad shit.*

The other squad members all felt the same way. Jackson had far too few days left to be included in the operation. No soldier in 'Nam wanted to get killed or wounded at any time, but especially not as a short-timer, with just a week or so left in-country and his long-awaited flight on the Freedom Bird back to the World within reach.

Short-timers felt the stress of combat more acutely than other soldiers. It was for this reason, and a sense of compassion, that company commanders in the field often sent them back to the rear and a much safer environment. The troops even came to expect it. Then again, mostly because of a shortage of soldiers, company commanders would sometimes opt to keep these men in the field until their last two or three days in-country. Weighing these factors, it could be a very tough call.

"It's gonna be dark before too long," Wilson resumed, "so we're gonna haul-ass." He turned to the grunt who had directed the chopper in. "McCracken, you're on point. Same order of march, but Scott and Arano will go in the middle. Charlie knows we're here, so keep your eyes and ears open."

As they formed into a file, some of the men welcomed Scott and Arano, but the new men also heard a few comments about "fuckin' new guys," which made them feel a little like freshmen among a pack of hot-shot seniors. Still, the older veterans saw the razzing as a *right-of-passage* for new troops, and no big deal.

The steep climb up the hill was every bit as tough as Wilson had noted. In fact, it was much more than "a bitch of a climb," especially for Scott and Arano. Bugs, leeches, spiders, the thick tangles of jungle growth and ensnaring vines, random patches of razor-sharp elephant grass, their equipment and heavy rucksacks, the stifling heat and humidity—all of it, the whole gamut of obstacles, seemed to conspire to make the climb as hard as possible to reach the summit.

Sergeant Wilson had placed Scott and Arano in the middle of the file, and of all the men, they had the most difficult time keeping up with the pace. Halfway up, a clap of thunder cracked across the gray sky, letting loose a torrential downpour. They expected Wilson would call a halt to give time to put on ponchos, but the sergeant kept the men moving through the short-lived downpour.

Soon after the rain stopped, however, Wilson called for a break. Scott and Arano flopped down in the thick jungle, exhausted, sitting upright in their soaked fatigues, with their backs resting against their rucksacks. They were gulping canteen water when Wilson came by to check on them.

"You guys hackin' it okay?" he asked.

"Yeah, Sarge," they responded, before drinking more water.

Wilson nodded. "Keep your eyes and ears open, and don't get too comfortable. We'll be movin' real soon." He started to leave, but stopped to add, "And go slow on the water. You won't find any more on the hilltop."

After Wilson left, Arano complained to Scott. "Keep your eyes open! *Ay, caramba*! This stuff is so thick you can't see three feet. Give me a break."

Just a few minutes later, Wilson called, "Saddle up, we're movin' out."

"*Madre mia*!" Arano cried in a low voice. "We just stopped!"

In moments, the hard, long hump up the obstacle-course-of-a hill resumed. *How in the hell,* Scott wondered, trudging along under the weight of his rucksack, *am I ever gonna make it through a year of this?* Suddenly, he had a lot more sympathy for Jackson and his short-timer's plight.

Scott's thoughts turned to home, and soon his troubling question came back to him like the clarion call of a church bell, ringing in his mind. *How in the hell am I ever gonna make it through a year of this?*

His inquiry was cut short when one of the men in the front of the file suddenly opened fire. The single burst was quickly followed by an exchange of gunfire, with two distinctly different sounds, one an AK-47, the other an M-16. Then all hell broke loose, as more AKs opened fire, and the grunts at the front of the file fired back. Scott and Arano went prone with their M-16's set to full-automatic, safety switches off and their nerves in knots. Arano wiped sweat from his eyes and pushed his helmet back off his forehead to see better.

"Grenade! Fire in the hole!" one of the grunts yelled, throwing a fragmentation grenade through the thick undergrowth toward the sound of the enemy firing. The other grunts ducked low as the grenade exploded, sending deadly shrapnel ripping through the jungle foliage, and setting off a loud ringing in their ears. Another grunt, tossed a second grenade, giving the same warning to his buddies.

"There!" Scott hollered, after the grenade exploded. He pointed to his front right, thinking he saw something move, then fired two short bursts from his rifle. Arano followed suit.

The firefight continued, but when the enemy suddenly broke it off, the grunts ceased firing, too. Ten minutes later, Wilson sent McCracken, his point man, out on a quick reconnaissance. After a short while, a burst from his M-16 shattered the stillness. It was followed by another short burst, then quiet resumed. When the point man soon returned, he carried an AK-47 he had taken from a dead man.

"One dead-ass Victor Charlie up ahead, Sarge," the grunt reported to Wilson. "Saw blood trails, but nothin' else."

A radio call from the First Platoon leader, Lieutenant Hinton, up on the hilltop, interrupted the report. He wanted to know about the firing, and the sergeant quickly gave him the situation report, also informing him that the squad would be back on the move shortly. Hinton gave him a new azimuth to follow, for a slightly different route back up the hill. On signing off, the sergeant checked his compass and had his point man set out on the new course. They hadn't gone far when they came to the body of the dead VC. Much of his upper torso and part of his face and head had been ripped away.

The squad bunched up around the black pajama clad body, giving Scott and Arano their first look at a dead enemy soldier. And as many of them as the older veterans had seen, they still had a morbid curiosity for a dead soldier.

"Dude looks like a teenager," one of the men said in surprise. "Damn! He might be younger than us."

"Teenager or not," another said, "he won't be shootin' at us anymore."

Jackson stepped forward and quietly flipped an Ace of Spades down on the dead man's chest. "Sorry 'bout that," he muttered, as Wilson called for the squad to get back on the move.

From that point on, to the top of the hill, both Scott and Arano thought mostly about the dead man. They wondered about his family, how he came to join ranks with the Viet Cong. Did he have a girlfriend or a wife back in his village? How strange it was that of all the places in the world, fate had led him to this particular hill on this particular day at this particular hour only to meet his death. *It's crazy hard to comprehend*, Scott thought. *Crazy hard.*

. . .

Victor 60, the mobile Command Post (CP) went into action immediately upon its arrival. The police established communications between the post's base radio set and all elements of the team. Now Captain Rutkowski was able to better command and coordinate the operation. Separated internally by sliding glass doors, Victor 60 consisted of two distinct sections. The first room was the actual CP with a full complement of office equipment. The hostage negotiations team utilized the second room on the other side of the glass doors.

Inside the CP, Lieutenant Manly reported to Rutkowski that an automobile accident had occurred nearby, up at Fourth and Market Streets, at the intersection where the barricade had been set up.

"A drunk driver slammed into the back of a car waiting at the traffic light on Fourth," Manly explained. "Our guys were right on it."

"Anyone injured? None of ours, I hope."

"No, all civilians! Two critically, with the driver getting off with only minor injuries. Ambulance should be getting there soon."

Rutkowski shook his head. "Sorry about the injured, but let's hope none of this upsets Scott."

Manly nodded. "I was thinking the same thing, Captain."

Rutkowski spoke on the phone with the department's legal counsel, who was always ready to dispense advice to operation's leaders. The Hostage Negotiations team interviewed Kathy Hamilton and Arthur and Julie Benedict.

"So, let me lay out what we have going here," Lieutenant Nora Henderson said, standing at the white board, grease pen in hand. On the board, in large black print, she had written the names: Kathy Hamilton, girlfriend. Arthur Benedict, VA Psychologist. Julie Benedict, RN.

"Brian Scott," she went on, "is a distraught war veteran, perhaps suffering with PTSD, has a gun, and has threatened suicide. He's holding three hostages inside McGuiggan's Pub. Correct?"

Lieutenant Manly nodded, "That's the situation, Lieutenant," he said. Kathy and the Benedicts, seated in front of Henderson, agreed. Julie and Arthur each held one of Kathy's hands, trying to comfort her.

"Has Scott ever threatened suicide before?" Henderson asked, brushing strands of blond hair back off her forehead.

Kathy quickly spoke up. "No, not that I know of. Until a few days ago, he never gave any indication that he could do anything like this."

"Never threatened anyone else?"

"No," said Kathy. "He's a kind, gentle man, Lieutenant."

"Okay," Henderson said. "So, all of this is completely out of character for him. And I've been informed that he's in McGuiggan's relating some sort of story about Vietnam to his hostages, and that when he's finished, he'll talk with us. Correct?"

"Yes, that's correct," Manly said, nodding. "And that's pretty much everything we have."

The entrance door to Victor 60 suddenly opened and a patrol officer led Brian Scott, Sr. inside to see Captain Rutkowski.

"I'm trying to decide if we should attempt another call to Brian," Lieutenant Henderson went on. "And if we do, which one of you would be best suited to talk with him. I'm leaning toward you, Ms. Hamilton."

Kathy was about to speak when Mr. Scott, having overheard, suddenly pushed forward. "No," he demanded. "I don't want her speaking to my son!"

All heads turned toward him. Captain Rutkowski hung up the telephone, while Kathy felt suddenly sick to her stomach and sunk down in her chair.

"And who are you, sir?" Henderson quickly asked.

"I'm Brian Scott's father. I don't think Miss Hamilton should be the one to talk with Brian. It must be me. I have to talk with him!"

Regaining her grit and composure, Kathy jumped up from her chair. "On the contrary, I think you'd be the very last person Brian would want to talk to right now."

"I didn't come here to argue," Mr. Scott said, softening. "I came to help save my son." He lowered his head slightly. "I apologize for the things I've said to you, Miss Hamilton. You were right. I know that much of this is my fault. If only I had done things differently with Brian. If only we had talked more. If only, if only …" His voice faltered and broke off. The room went silent for a few moments before he spoke again.

"I don't have much life left in me, and I have a lot to make up for. I'm going to start tonight. So, I simply must talk with Brian. I must tell him some things."

Henderson smiled cordially. "I understand, Mr. Scott," she said, "and thank you for coming. Now if you'd please have a seat." She turned to the white board and wrote, "Brian Scott, Sr./father." The process of picking the right person to aid in the negotiations had just become a bit more complicated.

CHAPTER 15

In McGuiggan's Pub, Brian went on with his story:

Sergeant Wilson's squad made it to the hilltop within an hour after the firefight on the hillside had ended. As the squad walked through the company's foxhole perimeter, dirty, sweat-soaked grunts by their foxholes held their fire, while some came forward to welcome Jackson back.

"Hey, Short-timer," a grunt called, "how's it hangin', man?"

"What do you know?" another said, "Victor Charlie's worst nightmare is back in the saddle."

And still another asked with a laugh, "Yo, D-Ray, did ya get any boom-boom while you were shamin' back in the rear?" This one brought a laugh from the others.

There were a few comments about the two new guys, too, but Scott and Arano ignored them and just kept walking. When they were well within the company's defensive perimeter, Sergeant Wilson had his squad return to their foxholes, all except for Scott and Arano. Breathing hard and sweating profusely, they knelt to get a much-needed rest. Their training had barely prepared them for the rigors of this first day in the bush. Both felt drained and queasy in their stomachs. Wilson led them to a spot near the center of the perimeter, where the company commander had set up his command post for the night.

Captain Joseph Minner was a career officer and had been the commander of Bravo Company for just over five months. In regard to service in the field, he was a short-timer himself, since Army officers normally spent only six months in the bush, while regular soldiers spent twelve. As per military protocol, Scott and Arano saluted the Old Man upon meeting him. They found him to be welcoming and friendly, as well as deliberate and firm.

"I'm assigning you two to the Second Platoon," Minner informed them. "Right now, they're the most shorthanded and have the greatest need for replacements." He turned to Sergeant Wilson, who quickly concurred.

"That's a rog, sir," Wilson said. "We can use 'em. And remember, we're losing Jackson shortly."

"That's right," the Captain said. "So, you men will greatly add to our combat effectiveness."

Minner briefly explained the current Search and Destroy Operation the company was conducting in the valley, saying that Alpha and Charlie companies were taking part too, but were currently a couple klicks to the north. He said the area has been a VC stronghold, and that NVA units have been active here, too. Scott and Arano hung on his every word and knew they had landed in a not so good place. Yet, they had some things to be thankful for— they were alive and were going to the same platoon.

Afterward, Sergeant Wilson took them to meet the Second Platoon Leader, Lieutenant Hinton, who once again welcomed the men to the platoon. They were hoping to be placed into Wilson's squad since they already knew him and his men, but the Lieutenant instead put them in the 3rd squad, which had fewer men.

Finally, Wilson introduced them to their new squad leader, Buck Sergeant, Ronnie Felton, another seasoned grunt. Afterward, Wilson left them.

"It's gettin' dark," Felton said to them. "There's no time to stand here and shoot the shit. If we have time, we can talk in the morning. We'll be movin' back into the valley at sunup. Right now, you guys need to get in a position for the night. So, follow me."

Felton led the two through the hacked down jungle growth to the portion of the perimeter line where the 3rd squad grunts began and were already in two-man foxhole positions, which were spread fifteen to twenty feet or so apart. He led Scott and Arano past each position, checking on his men as he went. Finally, he came to the squad's last position, where a lone grunt with his shirt off and an O. D. green bandana around his neck was busily digging a foxhole and filling sandbags with his entrenching tool.

"Here's a couple new guys for ya, D-Ray," Felton said.

Danny Ray Jackson turned to see his squad leader with Scott and Arano! His sour expression telegraphed his dissatisfaction.

"No fuckin' way!" he complained, throwing his shovel down. "Ya ain't a stickin' me with them two, Felton. Put 'em some where's else. I ain't a havin' 'em with me."

Scott quickly said to Felton, "We can go to another position."

But Felton wasn't having it. "There isn't another position that needs you guys. I put Jackson here by himself knowin' you guys were back talkin' to the Old Man." He turned to Jackson. "Every other foxhole has enough men for the night, D-Ray. You either take these guys, or you'll be spending the night by yourself, one-hundred percent alert, with no sleep."

"Fine with me," Jackson barked. "I'd rather be by myself than have these two new guys."

Felton considered it for a moment, then said, "There's no way you'd stay awake all night. I'm puttin' these guys here with you whether you like it or not."

"Ain't this a kick in the ass!" Jackson griped.

"Think of it this way," Felton said. "Most every foxhole on the line has two men; you have three! Means you'll get more sack time." The squad leader turned to Scott and Arano. "You guys listen to Jackson. He knows his shit better than most. And when you're on watch, stay awake! Fall asleep, and Charlie might cut your throat."

When Felton left, Jackson climbed out of the foxhole and drank thirstily from his canteen. "Go on and drop yer rucksacks," he said to Scott and Arano, "and git to finishin' this here foxhole. Yer gonna have to make it big enough for three now. Sandbag the front, too."

Without a word, the two went straight to work. Jackson opened a can of C-rations and sat in the matted brush behind the foxhole, eating his evening chow and watching the two work. When the foxhole was to his liking, with a double layer of sandbags in front, he had the men stop and put out claymore mines in front of the foxhole. When they finished, he said, "Now chow down. We'll be pullin' watch real soon."

Scott and Arano sat and ate C rations and drank canteen water. They were reluctant to talk in front of Jackson, so they ate in silence with an array of thoughts running through their heads—home, the war, the two Vietnamese Jackson shot in that hot, smelly hooch, the Viet Cong teenager who died on the hillside, and how these things and far more like them to come were going to be their lives for the next twelve months. But inevitably, their thoughts turned to Jackson. It was hard for them to comprehend that right there with them was a man about to go home, back to the World! *If only it could be me*, they each thought.

In the fading light, Scott and Arano sat behind the foxhole, complaining about the leeches that had taken up residence on their scraped and bruised forearms. Amused, Jackson stood by, sharpening his bayonet on a stone, and watching them having little luck removing the ugly pests.

"Give 'em a squirt of skeeter 'pellent," Jackson said, "and the little suckers'll fall right off."

The two men tried it and sure enough, the leeches fell off.

But Jackson didn't let the lesson go by without adding something more. "Y'all don't sweat the small shit," he said. "Them leeches, the rain, the heat, they're all small shit. And the small shit ain't a-gonna kill ya or mess ya up, but Charlie will!"

Jackson went back to sharpening his bayonet, then stopped again, saying, "Ya best not be fallin' asleep on watch. Felton weren't bullshittin' ya. Charlie might sneak up on ya 'n cut yer throats. It's happened. And if'n you do fall asleep, and Charlie don't get ya, I'll git ya myself."

As tired as they were, having little to no sleep the night before on LZ Badger, the two assured Jackson they would stay awake and not fall asleep. His warning put the *Fear of Jackson* in them. Besides, falling asleep on guard would put them all in danger, as well as the other men in the company, too.

As darkness came on, Jackson gave the order of watch. Arano would take the first hour, Scott the second, and Jackson the third. Watch was for one hour, with the man on duty sitting in the foxhole, behind the sandbags, eyes and ears open wide, with his M-16 at the ready and the claymore mine detonators in easy reach. If anything stirs in front of the foxhole, it's Charlie! Wake the others, blow a claymore, fire at will. In short, defend the position with everything you have. If the hour passes without incident, wake the next man to take over, then sack out. Pretty simple if each man stayed awake on his watch. At daybreak, everyone would be up, preparing to move out. It was the daily routine.

When Arano began the first watch, it was so dark he could barely see his hand in front of his face. Jackson and Scott were already asleep on the weed-choked, machete-hacked ground just behind the foxhole. Arano sat nervous and alert, clutching his M-16 with finger on the trigger, watching and listening to the muffled night sounds of the jungle. He couldn't see a thing in front, just the darkness, which by its nature steadily tried enticing him into closing his eyes and going to sleep. To his credit, however, he did not give in to it and put his will to work to defeat it. He pinched himself repeatedly, silently changed position again and again, shooed mosquitos away, thought of his girlfriend back home, and their last nights together before he left for Vietnam. He even recalled the names of family pets long deceased. In short, he managed to work around his nearly overwhelming fatigue and stay awake.

His watch dragged on so incredibly slow that it felt more like ten hours, but when it finally ended, he quietly woke Scott, who was sleeping the sleep of the dead.

"What the hell?" Scott whispered, in frustrated amazement. "I just laid down! An hour couldn't have gone by so fast."

But it had, and Arano showed him the luminous dials of his wristwatch to prove it.

"Son of a bitch!" Scott muttered, rolling into the foxhole to take over the watch. In a minute, no more, Arano was on the ground behind the foxhole, fast asleep, holding his M-16 as if it were his girlfriend. Now, it was Scott's turn to go through the same anguishing, stay-awake ordeal that his friend had just completed. By using many of the very same techniques as Arano, he also succeeded in staving off sleep during his hour. The guard duty rotation continued through the long, weary night without incident, except for an hour or so of sudden rain (*small shit* as Jackson had put it). But shortly after 0200 hours, all that changed. During Arano's third watch, a furious firefight broke out some klicks away, up the valley. Arano listened to the tumultuous commotion, punctuated by helicopter gunships circling overhead and firing down into the jungle. Then came barrage after barrage of artillery rounds exploding. *Whoever it is*, he thought, *they're in one helluva firefight. Glad it's not us.*

Scott and Arano slept through it all and barely stirred. But as the firefight slackened, before it completely died out, Arano heard someone approaching from behind. Alarmed, he spun nervously around with his M-16, wondering if the enemy had somehow gotten inside the perimeter. Then he heard Felton's voice calling softly.

"Squad leader comin' in," Felton said. "Hold your fire! Squad leader comin' in."

Relieved, he lowered his rifle and allowed Felton to come forward.

"We're going on one hundred percent alert, Arano," he said in a rushed voice. "Get the others up! Old Man's orders. Everyone up on guard."

"Yeah, got it. But what's going on? I heard one hell of a firefight up the valley."

"Alpha and Charlie companies got hit hard. So, it's a hundred percent for the rest of the night. Anything changes, I'll let you guys know ASAP. Now get 'em up."

Felton turned and disappeared into the darkness, heading for the next foxhole.

Arano woke the others and explained what had happened. In no time, they were all in the foxhole, side by side, diligently watching and listening. Jackson put a plug of tobacco into his mouth. "Hundred percent alert," he complained. "Ain't this a bitch."

"So, a hundred percent alert means that for the rest of the night," Scott whispered, "all three of us have to be up?"

"There it is!" Jackson replied, then spit. "That's a rog. Yet, the Old Man could call it off, and if'n he does, we still might catch some more Zs before sunup, but I ain't a-countin' on it."

"Man oh man," Scott said, dejectedly. "We hardly had any sleep."

"*Hijole!*" Arano agreed. "How are we going to keep going without sleep?"

"Welcome to the 'Nam, boys!" Jackson said.

"Wonder what's going on with Alpha and Charlie up the valley?" Scott asked, wiping the sleep out of his eyes.

"Don't know," Jackson said. "But I gotta bad feelin' 'bout it."

Jackson's intuition was on the mark. Something was wrong indeed. A half an hour or so later, Felton paid another surprise visit to the foxhole.

"Listen up!" he said to the three men. "Get your shit together and saddle up. We're movin' out in fifteen."

Surprised, Jackson quickly spoke up, "Movin' out? The whole company?"

"Yeah, Old Man's orders. Alpha and Charley companies got hit hard somewhere north of us and we're movin' to a closer position to better support them at daybreak."

"Ain't this a bitch," Jackson muttered.

"Sorry about that!" Felton said. "Now, you guys get squared away and be ready to move out."

Felton quickly left for the next foxhole, and the three men went to work emptying the sandbags they had filled only a short while ago and stuffing the bags back into their rucksacks. Jackson sent Scott to the foxhole on their left and Arano to the one on their right, each with the same message to the grunts occupying them: *"Going out front to bring in claymores. Hold your fire! Don't shoot!"* Once they had delivered the message and returned, he had them follow the detonating wires from their foxhole to the two separate claymore mines, disarm them, and bring them back. After stowing them and the rest of their gear, they pulled on their heavy rucksacks and with M-16s in hand, waited for the order to move.

In the pitch black, Jackson gave Scott and Arano a warning. "Night moves are tough! Bad enough movin' a squad at night, let alone the whole damn company. We're gonna be walkin' up each other's ass to keep contact. So don't screw up! Ya hear?"

On their very first night in the bush, the two new men, knees shaking and hearts pounding, were going to be integral links in a very difficult maneuver.

"No sweat, Jackson," Arano quickly said, sounding confident.

"We'll be fine," Scott agreed. "Don't worry about us."

They waited in silence for Felton to return. When the Squad Leader finally showed up, he quickly let them know the plan.

"Order of march is the same as before we formed this perimeter," he said, in a loud whisper. "So, the second platoon will be at the rear of the company file, and our squad will be at the end of our platoon. Dead ass last! So, Jackson, I want you on rear guard, the last man in the entire file. Arano, you'll be in front of him, and Scott in front of Arano. Got it?"

Jackson didn't like the plan one bit. "That's bullshit, Felton!" he complained.

"Look, I'd rather have you at the rear than anyone else," the squad leader said, sounding almost apologetic. "Especially for this crazy ass move. But I don't have time to argue."

No sooner had he said that, than one of the grunts at the next foxhole called in a low voice, "Saddle up, we're movin'. Pass it on."

The squad leader quickly sent Scott to the next foxhole to pass on the information. When he returned, Felton was just leaving.

"This is gonna be one nightmare of a move," Felton predicted. "It's gonna take time and a lot of coordination to get the whole company into a file, but when we finally get movin', keep quiet as best you can. And keep contact with the man in front of you." With that advice, he hurried off.

It was another case of the Army's old hurry-up-and-wait game, for as things turned out, Felton was right. It took more time than had been hoped for the officers, NCOs, and squad leaders to get the

113

entire company of grunts, over one-hundred men, into a tight, front-to-back single file in the pitch dark. But when the confusion abated and all was ready, the order to move out finally came.

"Remember what I told y'all," Jackson whispered to Scott and Arano. "Don't lose contact with the guy in front of ya. Hold on to his pecker and walk up his ass, if'n ya have to, but don't lose contact—'cause we'll be in a world a shit if'n ya do!"

CHAPTER 16

Brian turned away from his listeners in the pub and abruptly stopped his narrative. Ashen-faced and sweaty, he trembled with the terrible guilt of what he was about to reveal. He couldn't stop his hands from shaking, and his .45 semi-automatic rattled against the tabletop. The hostages watched his every move, filled with worry for themselves and for Brian. Then suddenly, he pounded his fist on the table with a frightening boom, sending shockwaves of fear through each of them.

"Somehow, as I went through my year in the war," he said, "in too many ways, I became a lot like the Death Ray—which I never would have thought possible. And like him, before I came home, the new guys looked up to me to show them the ropes, too. I did the best I could."

He wiped a hand across his watery eyes, while the others sat motionless, hanging on his every word, and waiting on the next revelation with a kind of sympathetic sadness and voyeuristic curiosity. When he rested his forehead on the table, they exchanged glances, knowing that some terrible horror was coming.

Finally, he raised his head and pounded a fist on the table again, and painfully confessed, "I made a dumb-ass, stupid, unforgivable mistake that night, my first night in the bush. I made an error that has haunted me every day since. Too ashamed to talk about it, too ashamed to admit it and live it down, but, but ..." His raspy, quivering voice abruptly broke off and, in his torment, he paused to get his breath. When he resumed, he spoke differently, more resigned and settled, saying, "But … but after tonight, it won't matter anymore."

Despite the restricting fear, Cheryl reached out and touched a gentle hand to his arm, conveying her heartfelt sympathy and understanding. "What is it that is torturing you so? What happened to you?"

He pulled his arm back from her touch, shaking with emotion. "I don't know how it happened," he muttered, "but I did just what Jackson warned us not to do—I lost contact with the guy in front of me, and Danny Ray, Raul, and I were left behind, stranded and cut off from the company, in the darkest damn jungle I ever saw. And it was all my fault, all my fault!"

Shaking uncontrollably, Brian stopped to regain his composure. When he finally resumed his account, now with his unforgivable sin exposed to the world, he swiftly drifted back into the pseudo reality of it, as if he were reliving it. His intensity and passion transfixed his listeners, and swept them in, leaving them completely engrossed.

. . .

With Herculean effort, the human chain of plodding grunts moved blindly, and not so quietly, through the murky jungle night. To keep contact, each man held onto the back of the rucksack of the man directly in front of him. Whenever a soldier lost his grip, which happened often, a kind of frenetic panic set in until he had quickly regained it. Everyone knew the consequences of losing contact.

Twisting this way and that, over rocks and fallen trees, down gullies and across ravines, one obstacle after another, the file of men moved steadily north. At the very head of the file, the point man, when the situation called, used his machete to hack out a passable trail through the thick growth. And despite the "quiet and no talking" order, which was meant to be strictly maintained, the grunts hurled more than a few curses into the dark whenever one fell or got hit by a swinging tree branch. With so many men, the movement itself projected an audible pitch all its own.

The pace went back and forth from fast to slow, to stop and go, to hurry and wait. At times the men thought they were playing the childhood game, Crack the Whip. Some stops were momentary, while some were longer and still others much longer until movement resumed. Dreamlike and surreal, the stopping and starting only worsened the men's fatigue, especially for Scott and Arano, who were new to it all and had had barely a minute of genuinely restful sleep in the last couple days.

"Keep contact," Jackson whispered forward to the two men after a quick series of abrupt stops and restarts. His eyes had adjusted to the cave-like darkness, nevertheless, most of the time, he couldn't see Arano or Scott.

After one extended and fatiguing stop, Jackson finally pushed Arano. "What the hell's goin' on?" he whispered. When Arano didn't reply, he pushed him again. "Arano, you okay?"

"Yeah, yeah," he finally muttered.

Jackson reached over Arano and grabbed Scott by the shoulder and shook him. "Scott!" he said in a low voice. "You okay? Everythin' all right?"

When Scott didn't reply, he shook him harder. "Scott! What the hell, man? Scott!"

Scott's eyes snapped open, as he returned from a dark, confusing tunnel of unconsciousness. His lapse was only a brief one, but a critical one.

"Scott, Scott!" Jackson continued. "We still stopped? Ya got contact?"

Emerging from his stupor in a panic, Scott grabbed for the man in front, but didn't feel him. Terrified, he reached further, then ran forward to find the missing man, pulling Arano and Jackson with him like a train. "Yo!" he called out. "Where are you?"

"Quiet!" Jackson yelped, shutting him up immediately. At that moment, Jackson, the man with just a few days left in-country, realized what Scott had done and what it meant to the three of them. The company had unknowingly moved on without them, leaving the very last three soldiers in the long file stranded. Without a map, compass, or radio, and only a few C rations and scant water in their canteens, they were alone to fend for themselves against the jungle and a strong, wily enemy who lurked everywhere waiting to kill them. It was a grunt's worst nightmare!

. . .

Outside the Wilmington pub, a helicopter suddenly clattered close by. Drawing nearer, it banked over MLK Boulevard and, with its bright spotlight shining earthward, soon came to a hover high over Second Street by McGuiggan's. At the CP, panic set in with the bird's surprising and aggravating intrusion. Captain Rutkowski rushed outside, with Dr. Benedict following.

Inside the pub, Brian looked up at the ceiling in bewilderment. "What the hell?" he shouted. "It's our Huey!" The chopper noise had put him in the jaws of two nightmares.

When Rutkowski and Dr. Benedict hit the street, the doctor was quick to point out. "The sound of that helicopter could be a real problem, Captain!" he shouted over the chopper noise.

"I don't need a doctor to recognize that," Rutkowski snapped angrily, staring up at the helicopter. "That's our police medevac! What the hell's going on?" he complained, then raced back into the CP.

Lieutenant Manly was on the radio, talking with Russ Vinton. The SWAT commander was livid. "Who in the hell called our medevac? You guys trying to push the guy off a cliff?"

Neither Manly nor anyone else in the CP knew why the department medevac helicopter had come, but aware of his Rutkowski Principle, the captain had a hunch. He took over for Manly, and in a moment, he was on the horn talking with the pilot himself, who quickly explained that he had been called to transport the critically injured automobile accident victims to the hospital.

"You're at the wrong site," Rutkowski shouted. "We've got a war veteran down here holding hostages. You're going to rattle him. The accident is further up Market Street. Move the hell away, ASAP. Move away, move away!"

"Roger, that!" the pilot said, while pitching the nose of the chopper down and accelerating forward. With a loud clatter from its rotor blades, the craft quickly banked onto its side, turning toward the Amtrak railway station.

Inside McGuiggan's, the staccato rap-rap-rap of the chopper shook the liquor bottles behind the bar. It shook Brian, too, driving him out of his chair and pointing his .45 at the ceiling as if he were aiming at or signaling to the chopper. The others shrank back from the table, each wondering: *Why in the world would they send a helicopter? What are they trying to do? Don't they know he's a war veteran?*

"Hey, we're down here," Brian shouted at the ceiling. "We're here, we're down here!" He fired two rounds into the ceiling, to signal the helicopter, succeeding only in bringing down a hail of decades old plaster around them. "Don't leave us! Don't leave!"

Paddy took cover under the tables. Cheryl screamed and covered her ears, as Mark pulled her to the floor and put a hand over her mouth. "It's okay," he whispered to her. "Quiet, be quiet."

"*Amigo* and I," Brian hollered, with tears streaming down his face, "we wanted to fire our M-16's into the air to alert the company and let them know where we were. But Jackson wouldn't let us. He said Charlie would find us first. So, we didn't. We didn't do anything. Nothing!"

. . .

Outside on Second Street, pressed close against the front of the building next to McGuiggan's, Russ Vinton heard the sharp report of the .45 semi-automatic. Within seconds, he was communicating the news to his entire SWAT team and to Rutkowski at the Command Post.

"Be advised, subject has fired his weapon!" he spoke calmly. "I say again, subject has fired his weapon." The dire message, heard by everyone in the CP, set off a radio exchange between Rutkowski and Vinton.

"We may have someone injured or dead, Frank. He fired two rounds. We have the ram with us. We can be inside in no time. I say we go. He's a shooter now. It's a new ball game!"

"No," Kathy screamed, "don't let them go in!" She quickly turned to Arthur. "If they go in there, they'll kill him. I know it. He'll never come out alive."

The psychologist agreed. "She's right!" he shouted to Rutkowski. "They can't go in. You can't let them."

"Nobody goes anywhere yet!" Rutkowski spoke assuredly into the mic. "We're going to try another phone call, Russ." He nodded to Henderson to get her team ready. The three hurried into the adjoining room. Mr. Scott followed, but Henderson quickly stopped him.

"Not yet, Mr. Scott," she said, firmly. "We'll let you know when we need you. Thank you." She pulled the sliding doors closed, as the captain continued talking with Vinton.

"Before you go storming in there, Russ," he said, "we're going to try to find out what happened. Hold your position and wait on my orders. I'll be right back at you."

"But ..." the SWAT commander said.

Rutkowski quickly cut him off. "But nothing, Russ," he shouted. "It's an order. Hold your position."

"Roger that, Captain!" Vinton quickly conceded. "Waiting on your orders."

Inside the pub, the telephone suddenly rang, jarring them again. Paddy looked up to Brian, asking, "Can I answer it?"

Brian glanced at the phone on the bar top and went back to the table. "Everyone up!" he shouted, bringing the others out from under the adjoined tables. He motioned them to sit down as the phone went on ringing.

"They'll want to know about the shooting," Paddy pointed out. "We'd better answer it."

Brian gave him a nod and Paddy went to the bar and picked up the receiver. "Hello!" he said, then fell silent, listening. "It's Paddy ... yeah, McGuiggan. No, no one's hurt, Officer Martin. Everyone's okay. It was the helicopter! Okay, I'll ask him." Paddy held the receiver away from his face, and said to Brian, "They want to talk with you."

Brian shook his head and barked, "No!"

"He said no," Paddy told the officer, then listened. "Okay." He held the phone away and spoke to Brian once more. "They want me to ask you again. They'd like to talk with you."

"I have nothing to say. When I'm done, everyone can leave. Tell the police to stay away. I don't want anyone getting hurt."

Paddy relayed the information to Martin, then once more went silent as he listened. In a few moments, he spoke to Brian once again, telling him, "Kathy Hamilton is outside. She loves you and is very worried about you. She wants to talk with you."

Brian lowered his head. "No, no, no … it's too late," he muttered. Then looking up at Paddy, he added, "No wait, tell her I'm sorry and … and that I love her." His eyes were red and swollen.

"Maybe you should talk with her," Cheryl said, softly. But Brian waved her off.

"He won't talk to her," Paddy told Martin. "But he said to tell her he's sorry and that he loves her, but he doesn't want to talk." Paddy went silent again, listening to the police officer, then he turned to Brian once more. "Your father is outside, too."

"I don't want to talk to him; I don't want to talk to anyone. Hang up the phone! Hang it up!"

Paddy relayed the information and hung up, then quietly returned to his chair.

CHAPTER 17

As Brian resumed his sad confession, it didn't take long for him to fall back into that mental zone where memory and reality merged. His listeners were quickly swept into the realism.

. . .

Danny Ray grabbed Scott by his web gear and yanked him to within a foot of his face. "Ya dumb-ass son of a bitch," he cursed. "I outta waste your sorry ass right here. Ya put us in a world of hurt!" He pulled a fist back and hit Scott square on the jaw, knocking him to the ground.

Arano quickly wedged himself between the two. "*Madre mía*, Jackson," he pleaded. "He didn't do it on purpose. We're both dead on our feet. I nodded off a few times, too. I know I did. Come on, man, lay the hell off."

The infuriated Jackson drew back in the dark, muttering obscenities at them and his bad luck. He cursed the Old Man, Captain Minner, for ignoring his short-timer status and making him stay in the bush instead of the safety of the rear.

Scott lay on the damp jungle floor, rubbing his aching jaw and burning inside with guilt and fear. *What have I done?* he thought. *Jackson is right, we're in a world of hurt. How are we ever going to get back to the company? Oh, Jesus, what have I done?*

Despite the danger, Danny Ray exploded in a quiet rant about the sorry turn of events—the shortest guy in 'Nam lost in the jungle with two know nothin' new guys, with no radio, no compass, no map, and little C-rations and water. He knew better than Scott and Arano what a dangerous predicament they were in. Luckily for the three, none of the enemy were near enough to hear him. When he finally stopped, Scott got back to his feet, and they all stood in stark silence as the seriousness of their situation sunk in. Finally, Arano spoke, "Maybe they'll figure out we're missing and come looking for us."

"Ain't a-gonna happen," Jackson scoffed. "They ain't a-gonna come back, least not any time soon. Them boys are on a mission! And it'd be no good for us ta go stompin' off after 'em in the dark. Either Charlie'd git us or our guys would zap us. Best ta stay put rat here 'til daybreak." He punctuated his plan by spitting tobacco juice.

With no argument from Scott or Arano, the three hunkered down in place to await daylight. Jackson had them sit in a close circle, near back-to-back, a micro-mini perimeter for the rest of the night. On high alert, with M-16s at the ready, they listened to the quiet jungle, for any sound indicating the approach of anyone or any animal. The 'skeeters', as Jackson called mosquitoes, attacked them with a vengeance, and they quickly doused on more Army issue repellent. Sometime later, a firefight erupted in the distance, somewhere up the valley, in the direction where it had come from earlier. Helicopter gunships arrived to rain fire and smoke down on the enemy. After they departed, exploding artillery rounds added to its intensity before it eventually died out.

Huddled together, Scott and Arano prayed that they'd find a way out of the mess.

Jackson spit tobacco juice, and whispered, "If'n we hear someone comin', y'all hold yer fire. Don't fire at nothin'. Hear?"

"Yeah," the two men whispered.

Arano added, "We'll wait on you."

"Make sure ya do," Jackson muttered. In a moment, he thought of something else and added, "Either of ya fall asleep, I'm gonna di-di outta here and leave ya to the jungle and Charlie. He'll have your heads on poles by mid-day fer sure. There it is! Bigger than shit, he will!"

Dead-ass tired, Scott and Arano swore they would stay awake and not fall asleep. Despite their best intentions, however, the darkness, the quiet and fatigue worked against them and on occasion both nodded off for brief periods. But it was fear, the great motivator, that roused them each time. Lucky for them, Jackson didn't notice or perhaps he did and decided to cut them some slack by ignoring it. He, of all people, knew first-hand the extreme difficulty of staying awake under such trying circumstances. It could be the hardest of challenges.

Just as the Short-timer had predicted, no one came looking for them and when first light finally broke, he told Scott and Arano to chow down.

"Go easy on yer C's and water," he warned them. "No way a tellin' when we'll git more." Getting up with his rifle, he added, "I'm gonna have a quick look-see around. Don't go a shootin' me when I come back." Then he walked off, disappearing into the jungle. As soon as he was gone, Scott and Arano pulled C-rations from their rucksacks and began eating. It was the first opportunity they had to talk without Jackson being near.

"Don't blame yourself so much for what happened," Arano said, knowing how bad his buddy felt. "Like I said, it could have happened to anyone! You know it!"

"Thanks, *Amigo*," Scott said, shaking his head, sorrowfully. "I know you're trying to make me feel better, but it's pretty damn bad."

"Yeah, well, he didn't have to slug you."

Scott rubbed his jaw. "I had it coming, man."

"We're going to get out of this. You'll see. The good Lord—and Jackson, the Death Ray—are going to get us through this. You'll see." Then, holding up his can of rations, he lightened the talk, complaining, "I hate these damn C-rats. Man, they're terrible!"

Just after the two had finished eating, they heard someone approaching. Sweating, they sat nervously ready to fire.

"Don't shoot!" Jackson called in a low whisper. "It's me."

Relieved, they lowered their rifles as he rejoined them. "Saddle up, we're movin' out!" he snapped.

With no argument or questions, Scott and Arano got to their feet and put on their rucksacks and helmets.

"I'm walkin' point," Jackson said. "Scott, you're behind me, and, Arano, you got the rear. Keep spread out, like they trained ya. If'n we hit a booby trap, it won't go killin' us all. We'll foller the company's trail. It shouldn't be hard ta track. But if'n we lose it, we'll keep the valley to our right and keep goin'. We'll find them boys."

Jackson put a plug of tobacco in his mouth and chewed. "Go easy on yer water. We'll be damn lucky to find any up here on the high ground." Then he paused and glanced quietly at the two. His rugged face seemed to soften, as he said, "Y'all think I'm a hard ass, and I can't blame ya." He spit, then went on, "Ya gotta be hardcore to survive this crazy, fuckin' war and all the shit it can throw at ya." He paused, looking at them and chewing. "Y'all stay calm. We'll git out of this here fix. We run into anythin', follow my command. It might save yer lives!" With that, he spit again. "Ok, ready?"

"Roger," the two said, nodding, feeling somewhat relieved that Jackson had calmed down and was resolved to getting out of the dire situation.

"Let's git gone!" Jackson said, shrugging his rucksack upward on his shoulders to a more comfortable spot.

With Jackson on point, Scott behind him a safe distance and Arano at the rear, the three grunts began their most dangerous journey. Jackson had little difficulty staying on the path that Bravo had trampled down through the jungle. It wasn't anywhere near as difficult to track as a wounded buck in the backwoods and thickets of his native West Virginia, with his Pa's hand-me-down 12 gauge. Moving at a good pace, the point man made sure to keep the valley on his right, and because the trail was just a few hours old, he wasn't as concerned about booby traps as he'd normally be when walking point. Nevertheless, he kept a wary eye out for signs of them, most especially trip wires.

Later in the morning, Jackson called a halt for a short break. Scott and Arano, aware of Jackson's warning, took barely a sip of water from their canteens. In just minutes, when Jackson was ready to resume, he called a brief huddle.

"Keep yer eyes peeled for any kind a clearin' to recon the valley," he told them. "We're makin' good time and we gotta be gettin' closer. Any luck, we'll spot 'em or some sign of their whereabouts. Got it?"

The two nodded. "Yeah, roger," they said.

A thin, green snake appeared from the brush and slithered past Arano's boot, causing him to flinch.

Jackson kicked it away. "Bamboo viper!" he said. "Don't sweat the small shit. 'Member? Ya'll watch out for Charlie."

Back on the move, with the cool of the night long gone, the brutal Vietnam heat was regaining its debilitating intensity. Sweat poured from each of them, soaking their fatigues. Jackson used his bandana to dry his eyes and face. As the craving for sleep had tortured them during the night, now it was the craving for water that tormented them. Jackson barely touched his canteen and continued to warn them to go easy on theirs.

At one point, he gave them a more forceful warning. "Ya'll run out a water," he said, "ya can die a thirst before ya git any a mine." And they knew he meant it.

Around 1000 hours, Arano felt nauseous. Keeping up became far more difficult for him. Finally, he was forced to stop. "Yo, Brian" he faintly called to Scott. "Hold up, man! I'm gettin' sick."

Brian alerted Jackson and the two went back to check on him.

"*Dios mio*! I feel like crap," Arano told them, in a slurred voice. "Where are the others?" He was sweating profusely and seemed confused. Jackson put a hand on his forehead.

"He's burnin' up," he muttered. "Git his rucksack off." Scott quickly removed his pack, and Jackson took off Raul's helmet. Then he and Scott helped him to a resting spot in the shade of a leafy tree, where they helped him to sit.

"My head," Arano said, rubbing his temples. "My head."

Jackson looked him over closely. "Might be a heat stroke comin' on. Ya got any water left?"

Arano didn't understand the question. Jackson pulled the sick man's canteen from his rucksack and checked. "Ya got a little," he said. He held the canteen to Arano's lips and helped him finish what was left—no more than a couple swallows.

"Lie back," Jackson said. "Lie back." He helped Arano settle back onto the jungle floor, using the ailing man's rucksack as a pillow for his head. Jackson pulled off his bandana and soaked it with his own canteen water, then gently wiped Raul's face. He lightly pressed the bandana to his forehead and left it there to help cool him.

Worried for his friend, Scott, nevertheless, was surprised to see a different side of the Death Ray. He handed Jackson his canteen, "Here, give him some of mine. I have some left."

Taking it, Jackson gave Arano little sips.

"Yer gonna be ok, *Amigo*," Jackson said. "After a rest in this here shade, yer gonna be good as new."

The men stayed in place for nearly an hour before Arano started to feel better.

"As long as we're here," Jackson said, "we might as well chow down."

He and Scott opened C-rations and ate. "You better eat somethin' too, Arano," Jackson said.

Arano nodded and sat up. In minutes, he was eating from a C-ration can, too.

It was strange for just the three of them to be there by themselves, so quiet and peaceful. Yet, they knew it was an illusion, and that at any moment the war might come crashing in on them. Like the sand encircling an oasis, grim death surrounded them on all sides.

A half-hour or so after the men had finished eating, Arano seemed fully recovered, and Jackson seemed less angry and more resolved.

"We're gonna find Bravo," he told Scott and Arano. "We're gonna find them boys and we're gonna git outta this. I'm too damn short fer this shit!"

Scott and Arano agreed. Jackson's confidence buoyed them both. *Jackson says we're going to make it, and he knows his stuff. We're going to find Bravo company. Damn straight we are! Jackson's going to get us through this.*

Finally, it was time for them to move on. "Ya sure yer okay?" Jackson said to Arano, while pulling on his rucksack.

"Yeah, I'm feeling fine now," he replied. "I think we stopped at just the right time, before it really got me."

"Thanks to Scott," Jackson said.

Scott shook his head. "That's a negative," he disagreed. "Thanks to you!"

Jackson grinned. "Let's git gone!"

Once again, Jackson walked point, Arano went next, and Scott had the rear. By noon the heat was far worse than it had been in the early morning. The flies and bugs carried out a relentless attack against them, and they swatted and shooed them away with annoying regularity. Jackson carried a machete on his rucksack, but only used it occasionally.

Every now and then, he would stop and turn back to Arano, looking for any signs of a relapse. But he was hanging in there and would signal so by giving a confident thumb's up.

Much later, Jackson saw a spot that might provide a good view of the valley below. Moving to it, the men hid in the thick growth above a sheer cliff, where they gazed across the valley.

"*Hijole!* Some view," Arano said, impressed with the sight. "Mountains and jungle for as far as you can see."

"Yeah," Jackson agreed. "But no sign of Bravo!"

At that very moment, a firefight erupted further north of them, up the valley, beneath the green canopy of jungle, a klick or more away.

"There's our sign!" Scott said. "Can't see shit, but it must be them!"

The shooting had begun with just a few bursts of automatic rifles, then grew to include more, then quiet returned altogether. The men waited, but after a few minutes, a barrage of explosions echoed down the valley—then, all hell broke loose, as a major firefight erupted, growing louder and more intense by the minute.

"Let's move!" Jackson snapped, hurrying away from the lookout point, and going toward the firefight. Maintaining safe intervals,

Scott and Arano fell in behind and followed him. They hadn't gone too far when Jackson abruptly stopped and dropped to a knee. He hand-signaled Scott and Arano to get down, too.

Somebody's coming! Scott thought, watching Jackson, but when he began to methodically look back and forth across the ground to his front, Scott became confused. *Did he drop something? What the hell is he looking for?*

The tension of the unknown put the spike of fear into the hearts of both new soldiers as they watched silently. For what seemed like forever, Jackson kept searching the ground with is eyes, and now his hands. *What's he looking for? Maybe something the company had dropped on its night move?*

Finally, he inched forward on his knees, then bending at the waist, lowered his face to the ground for a close look at something. Momentarily, he straightened up and waved them forward. Moving cautiously, they joined him.

"Lookee here," he said, pointing out a fine wire just inches off the ground. He gently pushed some of the foliage aside and showed them that the wire was attached to an American M-26 grenade anchored to the base of a small tree.

"Fuckin' Charlie!" he cursed, in a low voice. Then, he explained the booby trap to them, how the wire was attached to the partially pulled grenade pin and that a slight tug on the wire would pull it all the way out to arm the grenade, leaving just seconds before it exploded.

"If'n I'd tripped this mother," he said, "I'd a been forward when it went off, either killin' one of ya or both. This here ain't no small shit!"

Swallowing hard, Scott and Arano exchanged looks of horror and relief. *Thank you, Lord! Thank you, Death Ray!* Both men wondered, *what would have happened if I was on point?* It was a question they left unanswered.

"Y'all move back a piece," Jackson told them. "I'm gonna disarm this son-of-a-bitch. Now, git a move on!"

When they were back far enough, Jackson carefully placed a hand over the grenade, the pin and spoon, gripping them tightly to ensure the pin didn't come out. Then he cut the trip wire with his sharpened bayonet and pushed the pin all the way back in to disarm the grenade. He waved Scott and Arano forward and showed them the grenade, then hooked it to his web gear for safe keeping.

Afterward, in the same order, the threesome moved out, heading for the firefight, which grew louder and louder the closer they got to it. Trooping on, Scott and Arano thought about the booby trap and the carnage it could have caused.

An artillery barrage suddenly whined overhead, and each round crashed to earth with all the ferocity and destruction of a falling freight train.

Jackson held up momentarily. "Arty support for Bravo," he explained to Scott and Arano. "No doubt, the Old Man called it in."

The heavy howitzers, positioned on a high-ground firebase somewhere far behind them, sent a steady barrage of deadly rounds in support of the grunts on the ground. The intensity of the explosions and the horrific firefight pushed the fear and anxiety level of the new men even higher.

"Arty's a two-edged sword," Jackson said to them. "'Friendly fire can kill ya just as dead as Charlie can."

They huddled together as the barrage continued, and when it finally stopped, Jackson said, "Let's git!" and he started off at a faster pace.

Scott and Arano soon broke into a jog to keep up with him. Sweat oozed down their faces and seeped into their eyes, burning, and blurring their vision. The jungle, the weight of their rucksacks and the heat, all worked to impede them.

Jackson suddenly stopped and dropped to a knee. In a minute or so, he waved Scott and Arano forward. As they approached, he put a finger to his lips, signaling them to stay quiet. The men knelt quietly next to him.

"Shhh!" he whispered, pressing a finger to his lips once again.

Above the din of the firefight, and the circling Huey gunships, they heard Vietnamese voices jabbering up ahead, then the thump, thump, thump of mortar rounds being fired. Seconds later, there were explosions as each round landed in the valley.

"Mortar," Jackson whispered, pointing ahead. "Firin' on our guys." He paused to consider how best to proceed. Finally, he whispered, "Let's move back a piece to figure this out."

With Jackson leading, the three quietly retreated back, while another artillery barrage rained down on the mountainside beyond the mortar team. The loud explosions covered their retreat. Then, Arano snagged a root with his boot and fell to the ground, accidentally firing his rifle. The single round went harmlessly into the jungle. Jackson dropped to one knee. Arano, his faced flushed with embarrassment and fear, also took a knee, and Scott stopped, too. With hearts pounding, they prayed that the enemy hadn't heard the rifle shot. After enough time had passed and no one came to investigate, Jackson got up and resumed walking. At a safe distance, he stopped and waved his two-man force forward for a pow-wow.

CHAPTER 18

At the busy Police Command Post, relative calm had returned after the near disastrous incident with the medevac chopper, which had been called to transport the critically injured from the nearby accident site to the hospital. After coordinating with the EMTs and Paramedics at the scene, the pilot flew to a new location just a few blocks further up Market Street, beyond the barricade, where it landed in a large empty lot that had recently been cleared for a renewal project. The chopper noise in McGuiggan's went from loud to barely audible.

In the CP, Brian's father took Kathy aside. "Would you please step outside with me for a moment, Miss Hamilton? I have a few things I'd like to say to you."

Curious, Kathy turned to Lieutenant Henderson, who was talking with Arthur and Julie. "Excuse me, Lieutenant, we'll be just outside in case you need us."

Outside Victor 60, the light drizzle had stopped, and a handful of patrol officers milled about in their rain gear speaking to a detective in civilian attire.

"I want to apologize to you, Miss Hamilton," Mr. Scott began, sounding sincere. "I hope you can forgive me. I mistrusted you from the very beginning, and thought you were just some woman looking for a man to take care of her children. I know that's cold, but it's what I thought."

Kathy welcomed his words, and her heart softened. Quietly, she let him continue.

"I didn't realize that you loved Brian so much. And for that and everything else I've done in my nearsighted, calloused way, I'm sorry. Please forgive me."

"It's alright, Mr. Scott," Kathy said, letting him take her hand.

"I've made many mistakes in my life," he said, with an emotional quiver in his voice. "Far too many to tell you about. But by far the worst was what I did to Brian. I can't explain why I've been so cold and blind. When Brian needed help, I thought it was weakness. I said terrible things about him and other veterans. I realize that now."

Considering his honest apology, Kathy felt genuine sympathy for him. It made her think of her own mistakes as well.

"You're not alone, Mr. Scott," she said. "We've all made mistakes."

The old man smiled. "You're very kind. I now know why Brian thinks so highly of you. I told you that I am a veteran, too."

"Yes," said Kathy, nodding.

"I suffer the curse of all war veterans—the memories that stay forever. Over the years, I've dealt with mine through drinking, which has only brought on more problems."

"It's never too late to get help, Mr. Scott."

"I understand, but let me finish," he said, with a wave of his hand. After a short, emotional pause, he began again. "In addition to everything else, I've also felt resentment toward Brian. Oh hell, how can I best put this?" In speaking about something so personal and damning, he had great difficulty finding the right words.

Resentment toward Brian! Kathy said to herself. *What on earth does he mean?*

"I think," he said, "no, I know, that for some twisted reason, I blamed Brian for his mother's death, my dear wife, Helen. I've never said it straight up to him, but I'm afraid my actions did." He lowered his head in shame.

"Maybe you have done these things," she said, recognizing his sorrow, "and if we had time, I could go through some of my own mistakes, too. But there's more to us than our mistakes. It's about recognizing them and changing. And you've already changed."

The old man looked up into her bright, consoling eyes, and said, "Changed! How's that?"

"You're here, Mr. Scott! And that says a lot about your love for your son and the real you."

He lowered his head. "I don't want anything to happen to him. I don't want him to die. I only want to put my arms around him and tell him how sorry I am and that I love him more than anything else in the world."

"You'll have that opportunity," Kathy said, embracing him. "We both will!"

. . .

When Brian's father went back into the Command Post without Kathy, Arthur and Julie Benedict became alarmed. "Where's Kathy?" Arthur asked him.

"She decided to stay out a little longer for some air," he returned. "She's just outside the door."

The Benedicts quickly went outside to check on her. "Kathy, are you alright?" Julie asked.

Kathy nodded. "I'm okay. I just need to be by myself for a few minutes."

"Would you rather us go back inside?" Arthur said, not wanting to crowd her.

"No, it's alright. You two have been so kind. I don't know what I'd do without you. I'll never forget what great supports you've been through all of this."

Julie smiled. "That's what friends are for," she said. "I'm sure you'd do the same for us."

Arthur cleared his throat, then said, "This whole episode has made me reflect on my own life, about how love and friendship are the most important things in our lives. We just never take the time to tell our loved ones how important they really are to us." He pulled Julie close and kissed her gently, then leaned forward and kissed Kathy on her cheek.

In a few moments, the Benedicts left Kathy to herself and returned to the warmth of the CP. In her mind's eye, she suddenly recalled Charlotte, the elderly woman she and Brian met on the Rehoboth Beach boardwalk—the one who had photographed them embracing and smiling so happily. She recalled the way the woman had looked so admiringly at Brian and how she thanked him for showing such concern for her sick husband. Closing her eyes, Kathy could see and hear the woman tell her: "Hold on to that man of yours. He's got a good heart!"

Her thoughts turned again, flashing to her precious son, Zach, then to Brian's father, and finally to what Arthur Benedict had just said about love and friendship. She reached into her pocket and found the prayer card that Father Dario, the VA Chaplain, had given her. In the dim lighting, she raised it closer to her dampened eyes and prayed the *Divine Mercy* prayer slowly, taking each word to heart:

Eternal Father, in whom mercy is endless and the treasury of compassion inexhaustible, look kindly upon us and increase Your mercy in us, that in difficult moments we might not despair nor become despondent, but with great confidence submit ourselves to Your holy will, which is Love and Mercy itself.

"Amen," she whispered, briefly meditating on the sentiments— the sincere praise and earnest petitions. Finally, with the prayer resounding deep within her, she put the card back into her pocket and went into the CP.

CHAPTER 19

Inside McGuiggan's, Brian went on with his spellbinding narration:

When Scott and Arano joined Jackson, they knelt quietly alongside him, staying hidden in the jungle foliage.

"Y'all keep screwin' up," Jackson said in a low voice, "and yer gonna git us kilt fer sure. We lucked out. If they'd heard that gunshot, they woulda been on us."

With nothing to say in his defense, Arano hung his head.

"We're gonna take out that mortar," Jackson went on, confidently. "We can't do much about what else is goin' on, but we kin put a boot up the ass of that there mortar."

He began laying out his plan of attack when they heard a noise, someone approaching from the north.

"Shit," Jackson murmured, "they heard us!" Calmly, he quietly sent Scott crouching a short distance to his left flank, and Arano off to his right. Then, all three of them lay prone, unmoving, with their M-16s on full-automatic and fingers on triggers. They had no idea how many were coming. Tense seconds dragged by, when a lone figure finally came through the brush and stepped partially into view.

VC! Jackson sighted in on him, noting the conical hat, muddied black pajamas, pistol belt, web gear, ammo pouches, and most importantly, his AK which was pointed forward ready to fire.

Come on! Show yerselves, Jackson whispered, eager to see the next to follow. But when the VC drew closer and no one else appeared, Jackson fired a short burst into the unsuspecting Viet Cong, knocking him backward and killing him instantly. The very second Jackson had opened-up, Scott and Arano fired too. With adrenalin pumping, they looked to Jackson for what to do next. The West Virginian waved to them to stay in place.

After ten minutes ticked by, and no one else appeared, Jackson waved his teammates to join him.

"Y'all stay put, and don't be goin' nowhere," he instructed them. "I'm gonna go recon. Don't go a shootin' at anythin' less you kin see yer target—'cause it might be me comin' back. Roger?"

"Got it," they assured him.

Jackson nodded, then he crept forward. Scott and Arano covered him until he disappeared into the jungle brush. Within ten minutes or so, with the firefight still raging farther ahead, he crept back and huddled with them.

"No VC," he said. "Now we're gonna git that mortar." He pulled a grenade from his web gear, saying, "This here grenade's the one Charlie left for us in that booby trap. I'm gonna return it, and y'all are gonna cover me. Shoot anyone we run into. We're gonna charge that mortar tube. There may be one or two VC there for security. If so, they're yers. When I toss the grenade, y'all take cover, then we'll beat-feet back here on the double. Leave yer rucksacks here and get ready to haul ass!"

Jackson set the grenade down and pulled off his rucksack. Scott and Arano dropped theirs, too, as he slung his M-16 across his shoulders onto his back. Then he picked up the grenade and pulled the pin, keeping a tight grip on it and the spoon so it couldn't fly off and detonate.

He looked hard at his two comrades. "Y'all take a deep breath. Git the butterflies out an' no screw ups. Them friends of ours in the valley are countin' on us. Ya hear?"

Grim faced, the two men nodded.

"Okay, git ready," Jackson said. "If'n it goes bad, and I get shot or trip and drop this here grenade, don't stop 'cause there ain't agonna be no time. This sucker will blow in seconds. Got it?"

"Yeah," they assured him.

"Ok," he said. "Now spread out some and try ta stay on-line with me as we go." They moved away, one on either side of his flanks, making some space between them. When they were in position, Jackson gave the signal and walked off. They did their best to stay on-line with one another. When they got closer and clearly heard the thump, thump, thump of the mortar team dropping rounds into the tube and sending them aloft, they broke into a run. Coming into a clearing, they saw three unsuspecting VC grouped around a mortar tube set in a little dugout. Rushing nearer, one of the VC turned to see them. Arano and Scott opened fire, hitting him and knocking him down. Jackson tossed the grenade underhanded, like a softball pitcher, and hollered, "Fire in the hole! Git down!"

Simultaneously, the three grunts hit the dirt, face down, as the grenade exploded, sending deadly shrapnel whizzing in all directions. Seconds afterward, Jackson pulled his M-16 from his back, when to his surprise, another VC with an AK appeared from the jungle in front of the destroyed mortar site. The three grunts fired into the man, ripping his rifle in two and knocking him down into the foliage.

"Come on!" Jackson yelled. Turning, he took off like a sprinter, with Scott and Arano chasing after him, trying their best to keep up. When they came to their rucksacks, breathing hard, they stopped and quickly put them on. Then Jackson, fast walking, as if on a forced march, led them further away from the carnage they had left behind. The horrendous firefight up the valley continued, even growing in intensity.

When Jackson finally halted, they burrowed into the thick brush to hide. "We'll hide out here fer a spell," he whispered to them. "See if anyone follered. No noise!"

Slowly their heavy breathing returned to normal as they sat on high alert. The moment they had gone into hiding, though, fatigue returned with a vengeance, forcing Scott and Arano to struggle to keep awake. Staring into the wall of foliage surrounding them, and listening to the firefight lullaby in the distance, only made the task harder.

Around the half-hour mark, Jackson finally whispered, "Think we lucked out!"

Scott and Arano nodded thankfully. "We going to move?" Scott asked.

"Not yet," Jackson said. "I'm gonna recon again. See if we're gonna work our way down from this here spot or keep on the ridge. Either way we're likely to run into Charlie, or friendly fire. I'm thinkin' we should start down from here, but I wanna have a look-see first, maybe git a better fix on Bravo's position too. Keep yer eyes peeled and be ready to move when I git back. And don't shoot 'til ya git a visual on yer target. 'Member, don't go a-shootin' my ass."

Scott and Arano didn't like the idea of staying behind. "Why don't we all go?" Arano asked.

"Yeah," Scott agreed. "More eyes!"

"More chances for noise and bein' spotted!" Jackson objected. "No, y'all sit tight. I won't be long. No noise and keep yer eyes an' ears open. VC around, and maybe NVA, too."

Jackson crept off, keeping low with his finger on the trigger. Scott and Arano stayed as quiet as a couple of statues, watching and listening to the surroundings and the battle up the valley. But with Jackson gone, fear quickly set in. Now, they were too scared to fall asleep.

"You think that's Bravo up there in all that shit?" Arano finally whispered.

"Yeah," Scott murmured. "Gotta be."

"*Hijole*! I'm glad we're not there."

"I'd rather be there than here by ourselves. Bravo or not, we're heading there when Jackson gets back."

The two fell quiet, watching, listening, and thinking. Soon they heard a low voice speaking in Vietnamese, then another.

Viet Cong! They exchanged nervous glances.

139

Noiselessly, the two grunts raised their rifles, and listened to the muffled sounds of someone gently trampling through the jungle underbrush. As the sounds came nearer, Scott held up two fingers to Arano, who nodded in silence. *Two VC approaching.*

A sudden movement caught Arano's attention, and he shifted his eyes toward it. A smudge of black, a conical hat and the muzzle of an AK-47—he briefly glimpsed them passing by. Now, there was no doubt the Viet Cong were looking for them. In a few moments, they were gone and could no longer be heard. Scott and Arano breathed again.

I wish Jackson would get back! Scott thought.

He had no sooner hatched the wish, than two black-pajamaed VC crowded in with their AKs pointed at them. Surprised, with no time to react, they raised their hands and pleaded with their captors.

"Don't shoot," they repeated over and over. "Don't shoot!"

One of the VC kept his rifle on them, while the other, the older looking one, quickly took their weapons and tied their hands behind their backs with a rough, sinewy vine. The two Viet Cong babbled excitedly until the grunts were bound up good and tight. They hauled them to their feet and jabbed them with the muzzles of their AKs, forcing them to start walking. The older one snarled angrily at them.

And like that, on only their second day in the bush, Scott and Arano had been captured by a ruthless enemy known for their brutality and were being forced at gunpoint to retreat in the direction they had come, presumably to some deep, dark, godforsaken jungle prison where a fate beyond imagination awaited them.

Why didn't they just kill us? Where are they taking us? The two prisoners had no answers but knew, with painful certainty, that their predicament had taken a dreadful, unforeseen turn for the worse.

Being pushed and hurried, Scott tripped and fell on his face. The older VC shouted angrily at him. He kicked him and punched the barrel of his AK hard into Scott's side. He tried to get back on his feet, but the impatient VC yanked him up by the arm and pushed him forward with Arano.

Dear God, Scott prayed, *help us, help us! Bring the Death Ray down on these two!*

Momentarily, a F-4 Phantom jet screamed down from the sky and made a quick pass over the ridge, then turned sharply upward to disappear back into the sky. The roar was deafening. Then a second Phantom swooped down and, keeping on the trail of the first, it turned upward and disappeared, too.

In their wake, the two excited VC talked hurriedly to each other, then pushed Scott and Arano on faster and faster. They, more than the two Americans, knew what was about to fall! The lead jet approached again, roaring down from the sky. The frightened VC pushed their captives to the ground, and then they dropped to take cover. The VC curled into fetal positions and held their ears as the jet screeched in over the treetops and dropped its payload of napalm bombs, igniting the jungle behind them in an ever-expanding explosion of fire. In moments, the second jet shrieked down and dropped its napalm too, then zoomed upward like a fire-breathing dragon, following the first, and leaving the jungle engulfed in raging fire and noxious smoke.

Although badly shaken, the captors and prisoners survived. Only the brutal heat of the conflagration had touched them. Still, it took them some moments to recover from the shock. When Scott and Arano finally came around, they were still captives. Any hope of Jackson saving them went up in fire and smoke.

If we're going to get out of this, we'll have to do it ourselves. That realization hit Scott and Arano like a rifle buttstroke between the eyes. In training, they had learned that once captured, a prisoner's chances for escape diminish bit by bit with each passing minute. They knew they had to do something quick before their captors took them any further. But what could they do with their hands bound behind their backs?

The VC looked back at the total devastation, and for the first time, Scott and Arano had a good opportunity to look them over. The older guy looked to be in his mid-thirties. His face seemed frozen in a mean, nasty scowl, and his decayed teeth were the color of the tobacco juice Jackson spit. The other, the younger one, looked to be a teenager of seventeen or eighteen. His face was a smooth olive color, and not deeply weathered like the older man's. Both men were lean and slight of build. Both had straight, black hair, and wore black pajamas, pistol belts, and web gear with grenades. They also wore black bush hats, and Ho Chi Minh sandals, made from old automobile tires, on their rough, blackened feet.

What a pair! Scott thought. *I can't believe these two captured us. What piss-poor luck. My year here couldn't have started much worse.*

Prodding them with their rifles, the two got Scott and Arano moving again. The firefight behind them continued, but since the napalm strike, it had eased up considerably.

After twenty minutes or so of hard going, the VC stopped. Muttering angrily, they pushed Scott and Arano to the ground, then seemed to turn on one another, arguing over something. The older man pushed his partner and shouted at him. He pointed into the jungle and went on to seemingly berate the teenager.

Scott watched them closely, thinking, trying desperately to devise some way to escape. He twisted his wrists, back and forth, trying to loosen or break the vines, but they held. The situation appeared more and more hopeless, when he turned his head and caught a glimpse of movement by a stand of banana trees ten feet or so away, amid the jungle greenery.

God Almighty, it's him! Thank you, Lord! Thank you!

He wanted to shout for joy and scream it out loud to Arano, but he didn't flinch or move or say a word or change the doomed expression on his filthy, sweat-soaked face. He choked his surging excitement all down, keeping it inside, and quietly prayed for God's mercy!

The older VC suddenly jerked around as if he had heard something, too. Alarmed, he squinted nervously toward the banana trees. In a softened voice, he spoke to his comrade and pointed toward the spot. The two talked in hushed tones. The teenager seemed nervous and on edge. Then the older man crept away toward the trees, looking for signs that they had been followed. Scott held his breath and prayed, hoping that the wily enemy would not find Jackson. But after a short time, to Scott's great relief, the man returned by himself. He quickly spoke to his younger companion, who now seemed relieved. While they talked, the Death Ray struck like lightning!

With a rebel yell that would frighten the devil himself, and firing his M-16 from the hip, Jackson surged out of the brush and caught them all by surprise. The two prisoners rolled onto their stomachs to avoid being shot, while the rounds ripped into their captors, killing each before they hit the ground. The Death Ray had saved Scott and Arano from a long, hellish imprisonment, as a war pawn in a miserable Viet Cong jungle prison camp!

Wasting no time, Jackson pulled his bayonet and cut the vine from Scott's wrists, freeing him. Scott got to his feet and grabbed his M-16, while the West Virginian freed Arano.

Thank you, Lord! Thank you, Lord!

. . .

In McGuiggan's Pub, Brian surprised his captivated listeners when he suddenly stopped his narrative and began to weep. His tears came from deep within his dispirited soul. The hostages likened it to the painful sobbing of a bereaved parent who had just lost a child. It was so gut wrenching and sad to witness. Brian stumbled from the table with his handgun and leaned against the bar, crying all the while. At the table, the others watched intently, with great sorrow and sincere human empathy.

"While Jackson was cutting Arano loose," Brian sobbed, "the old Vietnamese guy suddenly raised his AK and shot Jackson." He paused, unable to continue. Finally, after a minute or so, he regained his composure enough to add, "Then I shot the guy. I emptied a magazine into him and kept killing him. I'm still killing him, every miserable day and night of my life!"

He lowered his head sorrowfully, as twenty-two years of pent-up guilt and anger roared out of him in a gush of tears. Cheryl, now crying herself, started up from the table to go and console him, but her boyfriend stopped her.

"No," Mark warned. "Leave him alone. Let him be."

143

In moments, Brian went on, "It was like I shot Jackson myself. Just like I pointed that AK at him and pulled the trigger. It was my fault! If I hadn't lost contact that night, it never would have happened. It was all my fault!"

He pointed his .45 at his reflection in the mirror behind the bar and fired. The loud report reverberated in their ears and continued to ring in their hearts long after the shattered mirror cascaded to the floor, bringing a half-dozen liquor bottles down with it. The hostages ducked under the table for cover.

"I killed him!" Brian shouted. "I killed Jackson—I killed the Short-timer!"

In his bitter tears, he announced his long pent-up confession again and again, for all the world to hear. When he finally stopped, the telephone on the bar top suddenly rang, startling them all. But none made a move to answer it.

. . .

Outside on Second Street, a charged-up Russ Vinton argued with Captain Rutkowski on the radio. The SWAT commander had brought up the battering ram and wanted permission to break into McGuiggan's. He and his men were eager to bring this standoff to an end.

"We gotta go, we gotta go!" Vinton yelled into his headset mic. "He's fired his weapon again."

Standing by in the CP and hearing Vinton's urgent request, Kathy Hamilton didn't wait for Rutkowski to reply. She pushed past Lieutenant Manly and shouted at the captain. "You can't go in there. You can't! You'll kill him. You'll kill him."

Rutkowski swiveled in his chair, shouting, "Get her out of here!" Manly grabbed Kathy by the arm and pulled her to the door. Arthur and Julie followed them outside.

"You listen to me, Russ!" Rutkowski hollered into the mic. "I want you to hold your position and wait on my orders. Do you roger? Hold your position and wait on my orders!"

Meanwhile, the negotiations team continued calling the pub, desperately hoping that someone would pick up the phone.

CHAPTER 20

"Can I answer it?" Paddy asked, after Brian had settled down. "They'll want to know about the gun shot."

Leaning against the bar, Brian nodded, and Paddy quickly went to the phone. "McGuiggan here," he said, then went silent as he listened. "The mirror ... he shot out the mirror ... everyone's fine, no one's hurt ... it was only the mirror. He's still telling us a story ... yes, a Vietnam story."

Brian interrupted, yelling, "Tell them I'm almost finished. Just a few minutes more, and I'll let everyone go. Now hang up the phone."

Paddy quickly relayed the information, then hung up and returned to the table with the others.

Lieutenant Henderson's team passed the information on to Rutkowski, and soon everyone in the area knew that the hostages would soon be freed. At the barricade on Fourth Street, the Public Information officer had her hands full keeping the media under control. Photographers and cameramen wanted access to the scene.

. . .

Still at the bar, Brian continued his account. "Danny Ray had been hit in the back, down close to his hip. Another round caught him higher up by his shoulder. Both wounds were bad, especially in front where they exited. Raul and I laid him over onto his side, and we dressed them as best we could. He was in a lot of pain, and his cries were terrible, but we had no morphine to give him. Screaming in agony, he held my arm and stared into my eyes. I kept telling him he was going to be all right, but I don't think he believed me because I didn't believe it myself.

"Arano dragged the two Vietnamese off a short distance, so they weren't lying there in front of us. I sat and rested Jackson's head on my lap. He pulled me closer to his face and told me to check the cargo pockets in his jungle pants. He didn't say why, but I did as he said, and found a rolled-up plastic accessory bag that came with C-rations. It was tied tight with a string. Inside it, I found a morphine syrette and quickly gave him the shot through his pants and into his thigh. He was thirsty and asked for water, so I dripped canteen water into his mouth. Somehow through it all, he gave me a half-smile. After the morphine, all the color went out of him, and he lay still and quiet. It was a nightmare!"

Pausing, Brian looked away, staring down the length of the bar. But after a minute or so, he turned back around to face his listeners. Drifting away, he resumed his narrative.

. . .

Darkness was beginning to envelop the bleak Vietnamese countryside. And after the shock of what had happened receded somewhat, Scott and Arano had not yet come up with a plan that could save Jackson and rescue them. One thing was obvious though—Jackson was in no shape to be moved. Finally, Arano hit on their one option.

"I'm going to go for help," he declared. "It's our only hope. I'll go back through the area where the jets napalmed, and down the ridge to where the firefight had been. Hopefully, I'll meet up with Bravo company. They must still be in the area. It's our only chance."

It was a gutsy call for a new guy. Scott sadly agreed. "There doesn't seem to be any other way, Raul," he said.

Arano got ready to move out. "I have a couple cans of Cs left," he said, looking thorough his rucksack. "I'll leave them with you. Just in case I don't make it."

"You'll make it, Raul, but take 'em for yourself. You'll need 'em."

"*Ni hablar!*" Arano objected. "No way!" and wouldn't change his mind.

Minutes later, when he was ready to go, Scott gave him a final warning. "Keep your head down, *Amigo*! Stay low and watch out for Charlie."

"Roger on that," Arano replied. "I'll get back with help as soon as I can. Take care of Jackson! I'm prayin' *muchas oraciones* he makes it." The West Virginian was unconscious and barely breathing.

"Me, too!" Scott responded. "*Mucho* prayers."

Then, with his M-16 at his hip, just like the Short-timer and the other *old heads*, Arano crept into the jungle and disappeared, leaving Scott and Jackson alone. His greatest fear was that he'd walk into an ambush, either enemy or friendly, and be shot dead in an instant. Still, despite the danger, he was determined to find the embattled Bravo company. Meanwhile, Scott, tended to the mangled, dying Jackson, hoping against hope that Arano would return with help.

Later, in the darkness of the night, Scott murmured prayer after prayer for Jackson, who remained still and silent, with his head resting in Scott's lap. At one point, Jackson awoke and complained about being cold. Scott pulled his poncho from his rucksack and covered him, but the mortally wounded man couldn't get warm enough. And later still, Jackson opened up to him, murmuring about his family in West Virginia, and their little home "just a piece up the road, at the far end of the holler along the crick." He described the colorful maples, aspens, and poplars that painted such a dazzling portrait of his life in the back country. He spoke too of his ma and pa and how much he loved and missed them. And in his agony, he seemed to find delight in the fond recollection of his ma's cooking— her biscuits and white gravy, the buckwheat pancakes and molasses, the cornbread and beans, and her baked ham and grits. His halting description was so painful to Scott, who held himself fully responsible for Jackson's dire predicament. Listening, it tore the very heart out of him.

Scott never once stopped Danny Ray from talking. *If the enemy hears him and they find us,* he thought, *so be it. I hope they kill us both.* But no one heard, and no one came. Scott kept praying, and the night dragged on like a dark curse.

"I don't understand this here war," Danny Ray muttered at one point. "I don't hate the Vietnamese. I don't hate 'em or anyone. But they've kilt and maimed so many of our guys, I show 'em no mercy. God'll judge me fer it. Ya think he'll understand?"

With tear-filled eyes, Scott replied, "Yeah, I'm sure of it."

Sometime before daybreak Jackson got worried that Scott was going to leave him there to die.

"Don't leave me, Scott!" he muttered. "I don't want to die alone."

"You're not going to die," Scott assured him. "And I'm not going anywhere until Raul gets back." Again and again, in between his whispered prayers, Scott promised he wouldn't leave, that he'd stay with him until help arrived. He consoled him as best as he could. As the sun was slowly rising, Jackson had a request, one that Scott could not refuse.

"I'm fixin' ta die," he whispered. "I know it, but I want ya ta promise me somethin'."

"No, no, you're not going to die," Scott insisted.

"Listen ... listen ... when you git outta this shithole and you're back in the World, promise me you'll visit my folks and tell 'em that I was a thinkin' of 'em when I died. Tell 'em I love 'em and all my kin, too. Will ya promise? Will ya?"

Scott continued to insist that he wasn't going to die, and that he could tell them himself when he got home. But Jackson, being Jackson, would not give it up until Scott had vowed to go to West Virginia.

"Ok, man," Scott finally conceded. "I'll go and I'll tell them. But mark my words, you're not going to die. I've been prayin' all night for you, and you're not going to die."

A slight smile showed on Jackson's pallid face. "I heared ya prayin' for me," he gasped. "I heared ya."

After this exchange, Jackson fell still and silent, and didn't utter another word.

Later, after daybreak, with Jackson's head still cradled in his lap, Scott fell into a deep sleep. Dog-assed tired, he could not stay awake any longer. Sometime afterward, two squads of 1st platoon, Bravo company grunts, led by Sergeant Wilson, with Arano on point, made their way to them. Arano ran to his buddy and woke him, while Wilson deployed his men in a tight perimeter around Jackson for security.

"*Amigo, Amigo,*" Scott cried on awaking. "You made it, man. Thank God!"

The happy reunion was short lived. Although Arano had told them all that had happened, Wilson and his men looked at Jackson's pale, lifeless form on the ground with stunned disbelief. He, after all, was Danny Ray, the Death Ray, the Short-timer, the one hardcore, badass, son of a bitch, who had earned every bit of his fearless reputation in the bush. Danny Ray Jackson! His mystique shattered by a Viet Cong gunner, who shot him in the back. They could hardly believe their eyes. The sorrowful, sobering sight brought out a pent-up anger and a visceral urge for revenge. Since the enemy had beat feet out of the area, there were none to take revenge on. Eventually, though, they turned their wrath in milder form on the two new guys, Scott and Arano!

The medic quickly checked Jackson. "He's still alive, but barely," he reported. "He's lost *beaucoup* blood. Scott said he gave him morphine. We're gonna need a dust-off, ASAP."

Wilson called for four volunteers to carry the wounded man. Scott and Arano were the first to speak up, but some of the others quickly objected.

"No way!" one of the grunts snarled, angrily.

"You guys ain't touchin' him," another growled.

Sergeant Wilson quickly stifled the resentment. "That's enough of that shit!" he barked. But it was obvious to him that the men all felt the same way.

Wilson quickly got four eager volunteers without the help of Scott and Arano, and under the watchful eye of the medic, they gently moved Jackson onto a poncho for transport to a nearby clearing for the medevac.

Sergeant Wilson called for his RTO, and quickly radioed for a chopper. Making sure one would be on standby, he gave tentative coordinates to the general area of the landing zone. Then, he pulled his men in from their security positions, and got them into a file for the move. To their satisfaction, he put Arano back on point and Scott behind him, assuredly the two most dangerous positions in the file. He placed the poncho bearers, carrying Jackson, in the middle of the file. When all was ready, he went forward to talk with his point man.

"Arano!" he said, getting his attention. "The open space we passed, with the dead mortar crew, remember it?"

"Yeah," Arano replied with a nod.

"That's where we're going. That's our LZ for the dust-off."

Wilson then ordered the patrol to move out. The poncho-bearers picked up Jackson, and Arano stepped off, heading for the clearing.

Except for occasional stops to give the poncho-bearers a rest, the patrol moved on unimpeded and without incident. It wasn't long before Arano came to the open space. The dead Vietnamese were already bloated in the heat of the morning. Ignoring them, Sergeant Wilson spread his men in a security perimeter around the clearing. Checking his map, he got the dust-off pilot on the horn and gave him the exact coordinates for the medevac.

"Dust-off's on the way!" he informed his men, handing the mic back to his RTO.

Now, unless the enemy suddenly hit them, it was a matter of waiting on the bird. As they hunkered down on high alert, the medic tended to Jackson, who had not regained consciousness. Scott and Arano, despite their pariah status, learned what had happened the day before—how Bravo Company had run into a large enemy force and had taken a lot of casualties, but had also killed many of the enemy. Now they were beating the bush with Charley and Alpha companies, looking for the remnants of the enemy.

Later, as the dust-off chopper drew near, Scott and Arano approached Sergeant Wilson, catching him by surprise.

"Excuse me, Sarge," Scott said.

"What's this about?" Wilson said, turning to them. "You guys should be back in position. What's wrong?"

"Nada," Arano said. "We've got something to ask you." He turned to Scott.

"We want to know," Scott muttered, "if we can help put Jackson on the chopper? We owe him that much."

Wilson looked at each of them, noting their penitent expressions. "I get it, men. I understand where you're coming from, but under the circumstances, I don't think that would be a good idea."

The two nodded knowingly, turned away without a word, and walked back to their position.

Wilson's RTO, who stood near the sergeant, watched them go. "Good call, Sarge," he said, smugly. "Those two have already screwed up enough!"

Minutes later, the chopper came into earshot, and Wilson was back on the horn, coordinating with the pilot.

"Pop smoke!" he called, and a designated grunt threw a smoke grenade to mark the LZ. In no time, the chopper circled over, banked, and came in like a descending cyclone, kicking up a torrent of dirt and green debris. One of Wilson's men stood in the LZ to help guide the pilot in. Like a pit crew, the men had Jackson loaded on board in seconds, and the bird was back in the air, on its way to the Evac Hospital in Chu Lai. The Short-timer's time in the bush had come to an end!

. . .

In McGuiggan's, Brian, with .45 in hand, lowered his head onto the bar and sobbed. The hostages watched, wishing there was something they could do to help lessen his suffering. When he stopped, he looked at them and added a postscript to his narration.

"After the company finally got out of that damn valley, we heard that Danny Ray had died in the medevac chopper before making it to Chu Lai. Then we heard he died at the Evac Hospital, and then, rumor had it, he died on the USS Sanctuary Hospital ship off the coast of 'Nam, on the very day he was set to fly back to the states. Wherever he died, the guys took it hard. They were hoping for a miracle that never came. They took it out on Raul and me, and soon after, we were transferred to Charlie Company, where the grunts didn't know anything about our horrendous first couple of days in the bush. We were glad to go, too. Raul and I stayed together, and we learned a lot about 'Nam, about killing, and staying alive. In so many ways, we became a lot like Jackson.

"Then about six months into our tour, Raul and I were on another Search and Destroy operation, southwest of Da Nang, deep in another jungle shit-hole. Raul was on point when his dark premonition came true. He walked into an ambush—tripped a booby trap and got shot in the chest at the same time." Scott fell silent, remembering his *Amigo* with great pain and sorrow.

"Both his legs were ripped away," he finally resumed, "but he died quick. I cried when we put him onto the dust-off chopper with other dead and wounded. Raul was my friend, a damn good soldier, and a good man." He lowered his head and cried sorrowfully. "And after I got home from the war," he added, "they called us all baby killers! Fuckin' baby killers!"

Going back to the table he took the pitcher of beer and filled his glass, quickly downing it.

"I'm tired of livin' with all this shit hangin' on me like a curse. At least I've finally come out with it, even if you are strangers."

He raised his .45 and motioned them toward the door. "Now, everybody out," he hollered. "Go on, get out!"

But to his surprise, not one of them moved. Looking at him, they stayed in their seats.

"Go on!" he shouted, angrily. "Get out! You're free to go."

Reluctantly, Paddy McGuiggan got up and started for the door. Mark took Cheryl by the arm. "Come on," he said, "we'd better go, too." They followed Paddy but had only gone a few steps when Cheryl pulled free of Mark's grip and turned to Scott.

"No, I'm not leaving!" she declared. "I can't. I can't let you do this, Brian. I just can't."

Paddy took his hand away from the door handle. He and Mark watched Cheryl go back to the table where they had been sitting.

"If I walk out of here," she said, "I'd never be able to face my brother when he comes home from the Gulf. I couldn't look him in the eye knowing that I didn't stay and try to stop you from harming yourself."

Mark moved to her side. "For all the same reasons," he said. "I can't leave either."

"And neither can I," said Paddy, also returning. "I have a lot of friends and customers who are veterans. Since I never served, I've always felt like I owed them something. It wouldn't be right to walk out. I couldn't face those people or myself. Besides, what you're about to do is just plain wrong."

Cheryl and Mark quickly agreed. "He's right!" they said.

But Brian was too mired in darkness to see the bright wisdom in that. To him, he had killed the Short-timer, and it was now time to pay for it. A life for a life!

"No, no, no!" he shouted, with tears streaming down his face. "Get out. I'm going to square things with Jackson. I promised myself I would." His .45 shook in his unsteady hand.

"But you promised to visit his folks in West Virginia," Mark said, "to tell them the things he wanted them to know. Did you keep that promise?"

Lowering his head, Brian admitted, "No! Because I'd have to tell them how he died, and I just couldn't do that, especially since I survived."

"But now you've come out with it all," said Mark. "You've freed yourself and don't have to do the terrible thing you're planning."

"Please don't," Cheryl pleaded. "Like Paddy said, it would be wrong. If you do anything, go to West Virginia like you promised. That's what you owe him."

"I can't!" Brian shouted, firing his .45 into the floor and sending sudden terror through the three hostages. Cheryl screamed and clapped her hands over her ears, trying to lessen the deafening sound.

"Get out!" Brian shouted, pointing his gun at them. "Leave, get out! Let me do what I have to do!"

. . .

153

Outside on the sidewalk, talking excitedly into his radio headset, Russ Vinton informed Captain Rutkowski, "He's fired again, Captain. We're out of time; we're going in!"

Not waiting for Rutkowski's reaction, Vinton called for the ram to be brought forward, and in seconds his men broke the door down, knocking it completely off its hinges and frightening the hostages even more. The entrance to the pub lay wide open and, with Vinton leading, the SWAT team stormed in through the breach like a tsunami.

"Everyone on the floor! Everyone down!" he shouted, with his rifle pointed at Brain. "On the floor!"

Brian remained at the bar, holding the .45 to his head.

The hostages immediately dropped to the floor as the remaining element of the SWAT team rushed in from the back of the room to cut off any chance of escape.

"Put down the gun, Mr. Scott," Vinton calmly said. "Please, put it down."

Staring blankly, his eyes wet with tears, Brian stood stone still, keeping the gun pressed to his temple, while a fierce clash between two competing ideas raged within him, the dominant one filled with darkness and the other with light.

"No one wants to see you get hurt," Vinton calmly said. "We want to help. We know you're a Vietnam vet, and we're thankful for your service. But, please, please let us help you."

As hardened as the SWAT lieutenant had become during his years of police work, Vinton absolutely detested the idea of having to shoot this troubled veteran, and he was determined to work his damnedest not to.

His hand shaking uncontrollably, Brian began a slow squeeze on the trigger. Vinton noticed that his trembling had suddenly worsened and he backed off a step to give him some space. Meanwhile, the moment Kathy Hamilton had learned of what was going on, she raced down Market Street to Second, determined to help Brian. She ran past the gathering of police officers at the corner, and nearly made it to McGuiggan's front door before Lieutenant Manly caught her from behind.

154

"Brian," she screamed, struggling to break free from the officer, "it's me, Kathy! I'm here. I love you! Brian, I love you!" Her voice echoed through the pub, surprising everyone.

Taking a huge gamble, Vinton lowered his rifle. "There are people outside who love you very much," he said to Scott. "Please ... for your sake and theirs, put down your gun."

His team members kept their weapons on Brian, knowing that the standoff had reached the critical point. If he were to suddenly turn his .45 on Vinton or anyone else, they would shoot him. That was the drill and what was expected of them.

"Please, put it down," Vinton repeated. "Whatever it is that's troubling you, let's close that door and open a new one that gets you help. You 'Nam vets are a tough lot. You can do it."

Lying on the floor, Cheryl cried out, "Danny Ray and Raul want you to live!"

A profound stillness settled over the room as the battle within Brian's chaotic mind continued to swing back and forth. He lowered the gun slightly, then in a sudden burst of perverse resolve, pushed the muzzle back up, causing the others to flinch with fear that the fateful moment had arrived. But after more seconds ticked by, the debate concluded with the bright light of truth winning out. With his head hung low, Brian set the gun down onto the bar top.

Ever so carefully, Lieutenant Vinton moved forward, picked up the weapon, and handed it back to one of his men. It was over!

CHAPTER 21

When they brought Brian out of the pub in handcuffs, Manly mercifully relaxed his hold on Kathy, and pulling away, she ran to him.

"I love you, Brian!" she sobbed, clinging to him with all her might. "I love you! You're going to be okay!"

Two burly cops quickly tore her away from him, allowing his escorts to continue to a waiting police car. But for a fleeting moment, she had held him, and in that sliver of time, their eyes had locked, and she saw a spark of light in his, and it filled her with hope.

Thank you, Lord. Thank you for sparing his life.

. . .

It took Captain Rutkowski an hour or so to finish at the CP on Market Street after his officers had taken Brian away. As procedure directed, they took him straight to the Delaware State Psychiatric Hospital in nearby New Castle for evaluation. Kathy was afforded no time to communicate with him after his arrest and before his hasty departure. Still, she was so relieved at the peaceful outcome.

"I will do everything in my power," Dr. Benedict assured her and Brian's father, "to get him transferred to the VA hospital as soon as possible. It's where he belongs."

The two thanked him and Julie for everything they had done.

Paddy McGuiggan, to his credit, refused to file any charges against Brian. Whether it was Paddy's example or not, Mark and

Cheryl also refused to press charges. The only concern they had was to see Brian get well. And on discovering Brian's torturous story, even the man who Brian threatened to shoot that night in front of his home refused to press charges against the veteran.

. . .

Driving back to police headquarters, Captain Rutkowski suddenly decided to make an unscheduled stop.

"Turn left up here on 4th, John," the captain said.

"Where are we going, Captain?" Manly replied, making the turn.

"It's not far; just up off of Lancaster Avenue," Rutkowski said, evasively. "I want to make a quick stop. I'll only be a few minutes."

He directed Manly to turn off Lancaster Avenue and go through the open cemetery gates. "Follow the road around to the right. It's just over the hill there."

Moments later, on Rutkowski's direction, he parked on the edge of the road and the two got out of the car. Against the darkened sky, the moon stood out so incredibly resplendent. Countless bright stars surrounded it, making the night atmosphere exceptionally pleasant.

"What a beautiful night!" Rutkowski remarked, looking skyward. "How many stars do you think are up there, John?"

Manly shrugged. "Beats me, Captain. Too many to count." The lieutenant couldn't help wondering why Rutkowski had come to the cemetery. *Certainly not to admire the night sky*, he thought.

As if Rutkowski had read his mind, he suddenly said, "My brother's buried here. KIA in Vietnam … 1969." He paused, then added, "He's been on my mind all night. I'll only be a minute."

Manly nodded respectfully. "Take your time, Captain."

He watched Rutkowski walk past the many moonlit headstones and finally stop at one, where he stood erect, with bowed head, praying and remembering.

Minutes later, he returned to the car, and Manly drove off, while his passenger sat in quiet reflection. Before reaching the exit, he turned to Manly and said, "My brother was a good soldier, John … and a damn good man."

157

Manly nodded, and replied, "They were all good men, Captain. Yes, sir, every one of 'em! "

. . .

In the days after the incident, Dr. Benedict was true to his word, and managed to have Brian transferred from state custody to the Psych Ward at the Veterans Hospital in Elsmere. Captain Rutkowski, Lieutenant Manly, and "General Patton" himself, Lieutenant Russ Vinton, were all instrumental in getting the case against Brian dropped. With Dr. Benedict's expert testimony on Post-Traumatic Stress Disorder and its long-term hold on Brian, along with the mitigating fact that not one of the hostages would press charges against the veteran, they had little difficulty convincing the District Attorney to drop the case and leave the matter to the VA healthcare system where it belonged. Both outcomes left Kathy Hamilton overwhelmed with joyful thanksgiving. She thanked them all for what they had done, most especially for their genuine concern for Brian. But, deep in her heart, she held her most profound thanks for the one who had so mercifully answered her prayers.

. . .

Of course, the gut-wrenching story Brian told in the bar that fateful Saturday night was communicated in its entirety and in detail by his three listeners to Captain Rutkowski, Dr. Benedict, and eventually to Kathy Hamilton and Brian's father. Captain Rutkowski used the information to better understand Brian's motivation for what he did. It provided Dr. Benedict with the necessary background to better comprehend Brian's psychological state, and it served as a crucial stepping-stone to more effective treatment and healing. Mr. Scott and Kathy, however, processed the information in a far different way, in a way that only a loved one could. For Mr. Scott, it made his estrangement with Brian all the more painful, yet, so providentially, it proved to be the catalyst that thawed the icy wall of bitterness and sorrow that stood between them. It rekindled the loving relationship between father and son.

For Kathy, the story provided viable answers to the many questions she had about Brian's troubled life. In short, it gave her a far greater understanding of him, and the profoundest sense of sympathy and compassion for someone she loved with all her heart.

. . .

On another Saturday night, weeks afterward, Mark Reader and Cheryl Mensinger attended a rock concert at the Grand Opera House in Wilmington, just six blocks up Market Street from McGuiggan's. At its conclusion, they decided to stop at the pub for a nightcap. Unlike the night Brian had appeared, the hour was much later, and many of the night crowd were still on hand.

Busy behind the bar, Paddy smiled the moment he saw them come in. Fate had brought the three of them together and they had formed a permanent bond of friendship. As they sat down at a table, Paddy came over with two glasses of their favorite draft beer. After greetings and small talk, he asked them, "Any news about Brian?"

Cheryl spoke right up, setting her glass down. "I talk with Kathy almost every day. She keeps me up to speed. What a wonderful lady. Brian's so lucky to have her in his corner."

Paddy and Mark quickly agreed, then Cheryl explained, "Brian's still in the VA, but he's expected to be discharged soon. The sooner the better, Kathy says. He'll continue seeing Dr. Benedict as an outpatient, but he's already made tremendous progress. He's eager to get his business back up and running."

Paddy nodded, and said, "I'll bet. Anything else?"

"No, not really" Cheryl said, sounding downbeat and looking less than overjoyed.

Paddy scratched his head. "With all the good news, why the long face? You should be smiling from ear to ear."

Mark agreed. "That's what I think, too!" He turned to Cheryl. "I know there's something bothering you. And I know it's about that night. So, out with it! Tell us what's wrong."

Cheryl glanced from one to the other, thoughtfully, then took a sip of her draft. "There is something bothering me," she admitted. "And it's been gnawing at me ever since that night."

159

"I knew it!" Mark said, proud of his intuitive abilities. "So, come on, what is it?"

"Yeah," Paddy said, "enough of the suspense."

Cheryl took another sip of beer. "Well, it's more of a question than anything else."

"So, what's your question?" Mark shot back.

Suddenly, she had an unexpected change of heart. "You know what?" she said. "On second thought, I'm going to keep quiet about this, at least for the time being. I'll tell you when the time is right."

"What the hell!" Mark cried, disappointedly. "You kick up all this suspense, and get our curiosity all worked up, then change your mind and refuse to talk about it. Come on, Cheryl!"

She smiled pleasantly and lifted her glass. "Hey, it's a woman's prerogative to change her mind. Remember? You guys will just have to live with it."

Annoyed, Mark shook his head.

"We'll, I'm going to leave you two alone to argue it out," Paddy said with a chuckle. "But, Cheryl, when you're ready to come out with whatever's on your mind, I'll be here. Now, I have to get back to work." Smiling, Paddy went back behind the bar, while Mark tried unsuccessfully to cajole the question out of her.

. . .

After leaving McGuiggan's, on their way back to Cheryl's place, Mark brought up the question again.

"It's just you and me now," he said, as he drove, "so what's the question you have about that night?"

Cheryl leaned back in her seat. "You really want to know, don't you?"

"Yeah, I'm curious as hell."

"Well, if I tell you, you have to keep it to yourself, at least for the time being. Promise?"

"Sure, it's a promise."

"Okay," she said. "Do you remember how Brian described Jackson getting shot, and how he sat up with him all night and into the next morning?"

"Yeah, sure," he replied. "How could I ever forget?"

She nodded, continuing, "And do you remember how he described the rescue and all of that?"

"Yeah," Mark said, "so get to your point. What's your question?"

She paused again. "So, my question is this—did Danny Ray actually die?"

"What the hell!" Mark snapped, almost running off the road. "Sure, he died. That's the whole problem, and why Brian felt so bad and got into all that PTSD stuff. I don't get you. Why would you ask such a question? What makes you think he didn't die?"

Shrugging, she glanced out the window and then back to him. "I'm not saying he didn't die. All I'm saying is he may *not* have died."

Mark swayed uncomfortably behind the wheel. "Ok, Sherlock," he snapped, "do you have any proof he didn't die?"

"No," she admitted, with a shake of her head. "And no need to get all worked up about it. I'm just trying to think this through."

Mark calmed himself. "Sorry."

"We don't have any proof he didn't die, that's true," she said, "but we don't have any proof that he did die either."

"Sure, we do! Brian told us he died. And he ought to know."

Cheryl shook her head to the contrary. "No," she said, "that's not what he said. He never said Jackson actually died!"

Frustrated, Mark raked a hand back through his hair, trying to recall exactly what Brian had said. Finally, it came to him. "Hey, you know, you might be right," he said. "I don't remember him actually saying that he died or that he saw him die."

"That's right. He never did," Cheryl said. "Remember, Brian said that they heard he had died on the helicopter, then at the hospital in Chu Lai. Then again, he said they'd heard he died on that hospital ship off the coast. So, which is true? Or what if none of them are true?"

The questions stunned Mark into silent thought. "You may be on to something," he finally admitted, "but it shouldn't be too hard to find out. Hell, Dr. Benedict should be able to get that information."

Cheryl nodded. "That's what I'm thinking, too. I'm going to call him on Monday, but I'm not going to say anything about this to Kathy until we get some answers. I sure wouldn't want it to get back to Brian, not at this point. But if Jackson's still alive, that's a game changer for him."

"I'll say!" Mark agreed.

. . .

On Monday, Cheryl called the VA Center around 9:00 a.m., but was unable to get through to Dr. Benedict. She called again at 10:30 and managed to catch him between patients. It didn't take her long to explain her question to him. His reaction was much the same as Mark's had been, but after going into more detail, Dr. Benedict quickly saw the merit in looking into it, to either prove or disprove her suspicion.

"Oh, thank you, Dr. Benedict."

"Well," he said, "if I didn't think it were worthwhile, I wouldn't be so accommodating. But if it's true, this could make quite a difference in Brian's treatment and his wellbeing. Quite a difference."

"I'm so glad you think so! But I have one other favor to ask of you, Doctor."

"And what would that be?" he asked, sounding a little surprised.

"Please don't mention this phone call to your wife," she said. "I know she works with Kathy and I'm afraid if she finds out and tells her, it will get back to Brian. And if my concern proves to be a false alarm, it could do more harm to him."

Dr. Benedict agreed. "You're absolutely right on that point. I don't think Julie will mind me keeping this from her until we find out."

. . .

By going through his normal, government-military medical networks, two weeks later, Dr. Benedict had the answer. It came via a fax from Mr. Robert Nedwick, an administrator at the Military Personnel Records Center in St. Louis.

Well, what do you know? he thought upon reading the brief document.

Later, that afternoon, when he had a moment, he called Cheryl Mensinger from his office.

"Oh, Dr. Benedict," she said, excitedly. "I've been on pins and needles waiting for your call. Did you find out? Was I right?"

"Yes, I did find out—but your assumption was incorrect."

Disappointed, she asked, "You mean Jackson did die?"

Dr. Benedict paused. "Yes. I received a fax today from the Records Center in St. Louis that confirms it. He died in Vietnam, just as Brian said. So even though Brian could not categorically verify his death, Jackson is indeed among the war dead. Case closed."

In silence, Cheryl pondered the news. Finally, Dr. Benedict said, "Are you still there?"

"Yes, yes," she replied. "Sorry, Doctor, just thinking. So, Jackson died on the Sanctuary hospital ship?"

"The information I have neither confirms nor denies that," he replied. "It doesn't say where or how exactly he died, only that he died in 1968 and is indeed listed among the war casualties for that year."

"Well, I guess that's that," she said, sounding disappointed. "Like you said—case closed."

"I'm afraid so," Doctor Benedict said, sympathetically. "But it was certainly worth checking, and I thank you for bringing it to my attention."

"You're welcome," she replied. "I just wish the results were different."

"And so do I."

"I'm not the doctor, but I'm guessing you won't bring this up to Brian?"

"No," he replied. "There's no need to. Nothing has changed. It's best to keep quiet."

Cheryl agreed and thanked Dr. Benedict for letting her know. Later that night, she told Mark about Dr. Benedict's findings. His disappointment was every bit the equal to hers.

163

"I can see why you wanted it kept secret," he said, admiring her foresight.

. . .

Brian Scott was discharged from the VA Hospital and he returned home to his apartment in Wilmington, to a quiet, curbside welcome from his neighbors and friends, some who were on hand the day of his breakdown and the terrible street scene with Kathy. The man Brian had threatened with his gun was there, too, and he wished the recovered veteran well.

"Sorry, man!" Brian said to the kindly neighbor. "I was really out of it that night!"

"It's ok," he replied, shaking Brian's outstretched hand. "It's ok."

Before his homecoming, Kathy had worked hard cleaning his apartment. She further added the female touch by garnishing it with fresh flowers and a *Welcome Home* sign. The place looked immaculate and felt so homey and welcoming when they went in together. A little surprised, Brian looked around thoughtfully, remembering his last time he was there.

"You're home now, Brian!" Kathy said, softly. "Thank God things have turned out so well."

Brian nodded and, noticing a crucifix she had hung on the wall above the archway leading to the dining room, he said, "Thank God for sure." He put his arms around her, adding, "And I thank Him for sending you into my life!"

He brushed a tear from her cheek, then pulled her tightly to him. "Thank you, Kathy Hamilton," he said softly. "You saved me from drowning. I love you more than anything."

Kathy smiled, and they kissed the kiss of the truly blessed!

CHAPTER 22

It didn't take Brian long to get his life back into gear. After some needed preparation, Scott's Welding went fully operational in no time. The work trickled in at first, but ramped up as the weeks went on. His relationship with Zach, Kathy's son, picked up right where it left off. Friday Pizza night became a weekly thing again.

Dr. Benedict continued to see Brian on an outpatient basis, but soon the psychiatrist extended the time between appointments. Naturally, some of Brian's dark feelings lingered. Most likely, they would be with him forever. After all, his memory was working fine, and memories brought feelings, both good and bad. Dr. Benedict helped him to better process and cope with the darker ones in a way that was more constructive, affirming, and less accusatory. In this area, he turned one in particular over to God.

. . .

Soon after returning to his apartment, Brian asked Kathy to marry him. Of course, she said *yes*! The plans had to be worked out, but the couple had similar ideas for a modest wedding. Shortly after their announcement, unbeknownst to them, or any of the others, something momentous was about to break. Like the sudden eruption of a long-dormant volcano, it came in the form of an unexpected fax from Mr. Robert Nedwick of Military Personnel Records. It was later in the afternoon when Dr. Benedict finally got around to checking his mail and noticed the fax. The letterhead drew his attention immediately. Standing by his desk, he read it with great interest.

"Good Lord!" He fell into his chair and read it a second time, and then once more. "Oh my God! They made a mistake … a mixup in names … Daniel P. Jackson for Daniel R. Jackson ... caught the error in a follow up review… sorry for any inconvenience." Astonished, he dropped the paper onto his desk, thinking, *Cheryl was right after all. Jackson is alive.*

After regaining his composure, he picked up the telephone.

. . .

On the following Friday night, the Benedicts had the happy couple to their home for an informal get-together to celebrate their engagement.

They sat in the kitchen, sipping wine, and talking about the wedding. But it wasn't long before Dr. Benedict brought up Brian's treatment and remarkable progress. He spoke a little about it to preface the revelation he was about to make.

"Now, Brian," he said, "there's something you need to know. I'm bringing this up to you as your friend, and not as your doctor. It's something we've only recently found out but waited to tell you until we positively had the facts. Now we do."

Brian had no idea what he was about to say. "Tell me what?" he asked, glancing at Kathy, then looking back to Arthur and Julie.

"It's about Danny Ray Jackson," Arthur said.

The name had an immediate impact on Brian, eliciting a look of surprise. "What about him?" he asked, leaning forward in his chair.

Beginning with the question that Cheryl Mensinger had raised, Dr. Benedict went on to explain how it led to his inquiry, and ultimately to the discovery that Jackson was still alive.

"He didn't die in that rescue helicopter," Arthur said, "or in the hospital at Chu Lai, or on that hospital ship. He came home from Vietnam and is living in West Virginia."

Brian sat in stunned disbelief, staring at Dr. Benedict. Finally, sitting bolt upright, he turned to Kathy. "Jackson's alive? He didn't die in 'Nam?" It seemed so hard for him to comprehend.

"Yes, that's right," she replied, taking his hands. "He survived the wounds he received there."

"I don't understand," Brian muttered, still looking a little confused. "Jackson's alive!"

Dr. Benedict spoke up, "I know it comes as quite the surprise, Brian, but it's a fact." He paused before going on to explain, "Jackson left Vietnam and spent months undergoing a series of surgeries, mostly on his upper back and shoulder, at Walter Reed Hospital in Washington, DC. Afterward, he was moved to the Veterans Hospital in Clarksburg, West Virginia, closer to his home. The gunshot wound to his lower back affected his ability to walk but, over time, that diminished too."

Brian sat back quietly in his chair. "He didn't die in 'Nam," he said, still trying to come to grips with the incredible news. He turned to Kathy, gazing into her radiant face. "He didn't die. He didn't die!"

"Yes, I know, Brian," she said, smiling softly. "It's wonderful news."

Brian turned back to Dr. Benedict. "You're sure of all this?"

"Absolutely certain," Dr. Benedict said, sounding genuinely confident. "I've been directly in contact with the Clarksburg Veterans Hospital. The news is confirmed and accurate. One-hundred percent!"

A sudden knock at the kitchen door interrupted the conversation. Dr. Benedict and Julie exchanged knowing glances.

"That'll be the others," he said. "Perfect timing."

Julie hurried to answer the door.

"Others?" Brian said, sounding more confused. He stood up in surprise as Julie let in Paddy, Mark and Cheryl. "What's going on here?"

"It's all good, Brian," Dr. Benedict said, smiling. "They wanted to be here with you tonight when we broke this news."

The three former hostages greeted Brian with smiles and handshakes—and a warm hug and a kiss on the cheek from Cheryl.

"We didn't want to miss this," Paddy said.

"Not for the world," added Cheryl. Mark nodded with a smile.

As the newcomers took seats around the table Julie poured more wine.

"This is turning into some night," Brian said.

Dr. Benedict stood with his wine glass. "Yes, it is, Brian. Now that we're all here, I propose a toast to you and Kathy and your upcoming wedding."

Everyone drank to the couple's health and happiness.

As Dr. Benedict took his seat, Brian said, "Thank you, Doc. Thank you all so much. I can't imagine any more surprises."

Dr. Benedict shook his head. "Well, there is something …"

Julie quickly interrupted him. "No, no," she said, then quickly turned to Brian. "There's just a bit more. But I think Kathy should tell you the rest."

Arthur quickly concurred.

Now, Kathy faced Brian. "There are just a couple more things." She paused for a moment, then explained, "When I learned the good news about Jackson, I did a little research myself. Hospital records are one thing, but I wanted to know more. So, I reached out to Jackson's family, and became long-distance friends with his mother and father, but most especially his sister, Sue Ellen."

"Sister," Brian said. "He has a sister?"

"Yes, and a brother, too. But he died in a hunting accident five years ago. Sue Ellen is married with four children. Jackson never married, but he's more than an uncle to her kids."

Brian interrupted, "And you never told me any of this?"

"No," she admitted. "I just thought it would be better to come out tonight with the other news about Jackson. Besides, I had no idea how Jackson's family would react to me. None. If it didn't go well, I never would have told you, and neither would any of us here. But they couldn't have been nicer, or more understanding. Sue Ellen is a peach."

Listening intently, Brian teared up over the news. Kathy paused to give him a moment.

"So go on and tell me," Brian finally said. "What else is there?"

"First and foremost," Kathy began, "Danny Ray Jackson never blamed you for what happened that night. Sue Ellen was certain about that. He told his family everything, and never once did he blame you."

Brian lowered his head. Kathy took his hand and squeezed it gently.

"Sue Ellen said that Danny Ray was a pretty rough cut. He'd been in a lot of scrapes with the law and that the Army had been good for him. It helped straighten him out. He never complained about it, at least not to his family. She said he was different when he came home, changed in ways she didn't expect. 'God works in mysterious ways,' Sue Ellen said more than a few times."

Brian interrupted, "Did he ever say anything about me?"

"Yes. He told her he thought of you often, and your friend, Arano—*Amigo*—and what happened that night, but he never blamed either of you. He told her that 'Nam was a brutal bitch', and the grunts were so sleep deprived they could fall asleep standing on their heads.'"

Brian nodded, knowingly.

"More importantly," she continued, "he told her how you sat up with him all that night with his head in your lap, and how you kept him warm and prayed for him, never falling asleep. He said your prayers kept him alive. He thought a lot about that during his time at Walter Reed. At the Clarksburg Hospital, he met a young chaplain who helped him a lot. Jackson opened up to him, and he started to pray. In time, he began to heal—emotionally, spiritually, and physically—which made his ma and pa so happy."

Kathy fell silent, giving Brian time to digest it all.

Finally, he looked up and said, "I wish Arano could hear this, too." No one spoke for a few moments. Then Brian added, "Is that everything?"

Dr. Benedict cleared his throat. "Yes," he said, with a smile. "That's it, and some story it is."

"I'll say," Cheryl added, with the others all agreeing.

Brian nodded. "Incredible news. After all these years, I find out Jackson's alive." He looked at Cheryl, then around to the others. "Thank you, all of you, thank you!"

"You're welcome," they replied in one voice.

Smiling, Paddy McGuiggan stood with his wine glass. "Here's to Brian and Kathy!"

The gathering cheerfully drank to the couple, and from that point on, the evening was filled with joy and thanksgiving.

CHAPTER 23

Close to a year after his discharge from the hospital, on a sunny Saturday afternoon, Brian Scott and Kathy Hamilton were married in a Nuptial Mass celebrated by Reverend Dario Renzetti in the ground floor chapel of the Veterans Hospital in Wilmington. Only family and a few close friends attended. At the rear of the chapel, a small gathering of curious housekeeping staff stopped in uninvited to witness the unusual hospital event.

Julie Benedict was the maid of honor. Brian's father was the best man, and Dr. Arthur Benedict was proud and overjoyed to give the beautiful bride away. Kathy, dressed in a lovely cream-colored dress, radiated her love for Brian through a joyous smile that, like her flowers, never wilted throughout the day. Zachery Hamilton made an exceptional usher, and everyone, especially Mrs. Brinkman, commented on how handsome he looked in his dark suit. Zach also doubled as the ring bearer. Danny Ray's sister, Sue Ellen, attended as a VIP guest. The middle-aged woman arrived just as the ceremony began, and took a seat in the back of the chapel among the joyful housekeeping staff.

After the ceremony, a small reception was held at McGuiggan's Pub, which had been closed to the public for the entire afternoon. Captain Rutkowski, Lieutenants Manly, Nora Henderson, and Commander Russ Vinton, accompanied by their spouses, all sat together.

Mark Reader and Cheryl Mensinger, recent newlyweds themselves, would not have missed the ceremony and celebration for the world. They sat with Paddy McGuiggan, who looked out of place in a snappy jacket and tie, while his Pub staff did the serving and bussed tables.

As the newlyweds came in through the front door, the guests stood and cheered. Julie Benedict gave them hugs and heartfelt congratulations. Then Brian's father stood on a chair next to the bar and tapped on his beer glass with a spoon to get everyone's attention. When quiet ensued, he proudly announced, "As Brian's best man, it's my great honor to make the toast."

Everyone applauded. Then he called for quiet. "Now," he began, "if everyone would please raise a glass—beer glass, wine glass, shot glass—it doesn't matter which."

A ripple of laughter went through the room as the guests complied.

With moistened eyes, Mr. Scott raised his glass and said, "Here's to a genuinely blessed couple, Kathy and Brian. May God grant them a long, happy life together. And may His peace rest within their hearts always."

The guests cheered, and the bride and groom kissed as everyone drank in the hope that those heartfelt petitions would be granted. Sue Ellen sat with Kathy and Brian, and they joyfully reviewed all that had happened over the last months.

One of the cooks stepped out of the kitchen and discreetly waved to Paddy. The pub owner quietly got up and joined the woman before they turned and disappeared into the kitchen. Sue Ellen moved her chair nearer to the bride and groom and spoke to them in a hushed tone. "I have a special gift for you," she said to the happy couple.

Brian and Kathy smiled politely but seeing nothing in her hands or on the table, they were a bit puzzled.

"Special gift?" Brian said.

"Yes," Sue Ellen replied. "Well, maybe I should have said special guest rather than gift." With a smile, she pointed to the back of the pub where, on that fateful February night, half of Lieutenant

172

Vinton's SWAT team swarmed in through the back door to help prevent a distraught veteran from harming himself. Brian and Kathy turned in unison, as if they were one, to see a beaming Paddy McGuiggan quietly leading a stranger into the pub. With the help of a cane, a tall, lean, hardened looking man with a reddish beard walked toward their table. "My brother," Sue Ellen said. "Danny Ray! He wouldn't come to the weddin' and would only come in here through the back door. He didn't want to make a fuss."

Brian nearly fell out of his seat. His eyes filled with tears of joy as he jumped up and greeted the Short-timer, like one who had come back from the grave.

"Jackson!" Brian said, shaking the man's hand.

"Scott!" Jackson said with a grin. "The new guy went and got himself hitched."

The two laughed, then hugged one another in a way that only thankful survivors of a great tragedy could do, filled with God's peace and joy.

"Welcome home, brother!" Jackson said.

"Welcome home, Short-timer!"

Keeping back, a teary-eyed Kathy looked on without interrupting them, knowing that Jackson's unannounced appearance was yet one more sign that their marriage had been ordained by grace. Brian finally led Jackson over to meet his bride. He gave Kathy a hug and a kiss on the cheek. "Ya got yerself a good one here, Kathy. Ya know he saved my life in 'Nam and helped set me on a better path."

Kathy nodded and thanked him for coming. "It means so much to us."

Jackson smiled. "And thank you fer the invite. Very kind of ya."

After they took seats at the table, it wasn't long before Brian and Jackson were talking about Vietnam. Brian told him about Arano.

"Sorry to hear it," Jackson said. "I know you two were close."

Brian nodded, then asked him about his health. "I'm doin' fine," Jackson said. "A hell of a lot better than when I first came home. I use this here cane to steady my walkin', but I could get by without it." He rapped the gnarled wooden cane against the wood floor.

Brian tried to apologize for the error he made that terrible night, but Jackson stopped him cold. "Ain't no need fer that, Brian. It was a long time ago." With a grin, he added, "Besides, a whole lotta good come out of it, includin' my third Purple Heart. That's somethin' to be proud of."

Brian smiled, thinking how there was so much more to the Short-timer than he ever gave him credit for. "It sure is, Jackson," he said, "it sure is."

. . .

Among the gifts the couple received, there was another that stood out as exceptionally noteworthy. It came jointly from Mark, Cheryl, and Paddy, who had been chosen to hand the special envelope to Brian.

Taking it with a smile, the groom said, "I better start this marriage off right." He turned and handed the envelope to Kathy, which drew laughter from the guests.

A hush came over the room as she removed what looked to be a letter. Unfolding it, she quietly read it to herself, while her eyes filled with tears.

"Tell everyone what it is, Kathy!" Cheryl called out to her. "Go on!"

Kathy dabbed her eyes with a handkerchief and held up the paper. "It's a gift certificate, for a five-night stay in the honeymoon suite of a bed and breakfast log cabin hideaway near Clarksburg, West Virginia."

Everyone in the pub, even the servers applauded loudly and lovingly. Then Sue Ellen came forward and handed Kathy a West Virginia roadmap.

"Ma and pa are gettin' along in their years," she said to her and Brian over the applause, "but they're plenty excited about meetin' y'all."

Kathy took the map and gave her a hug. "Thank you," she said. After a short pause, she added, "You were right."

"Right about what?" Sue Ellen replied.

174

Smiling broadly, Kathy pointed upward and said, "He really does work in mysterious ways!"

. . .

Before the celebration ended, unbeknownst to anyone in the pub, even Kathy, a sudden wave of emotion broke over Brian. For a few moments, he silently glanced around the room, looking at the joyous guests while thinking back in stark contrast to the bleak horror of the war. He turned to Jackson, remembering his hardcore demeanor, and thought of how it was with the rice paddies, the steep jungled mountains, the boobytraps, and the Godawful firefights. Someone walked past, and he thought of Raul Arano, his *Amigo*, and the others who had either died, were wounded, or maimed in some way by the bloody ordeal. Finally, he bowed his head, and said a short, silent prayer for all of them. Then, ever so thankfully, he looked up into the light, gazed into the eyes of his beautiful bride, and went on with his new-found life.

THE END

Dear Reader,

If you enjoyed this book, please consider writing a brief review and posting it on Amazon. Reviews are very helpful.

Also, please consider my other books, all award winners: *Jubal's Christmas Gift*, *The Treasure of Nonsense Woods*, and *The Allure of Twerpentnog*.

And finally, I invite you to visit my website— Dennis-skirvin.com and sign on to my Newsletter.

Thank You!

Sincerely,

Dennis D. Skirvin

Made in the USA
Middletown, DE
11 March 2023

26604106R00106